To Brittany,

It was great to see you and your Mom at the NAVC. I wish you much luck and success with your studies, and hope that you pursue your interest in

PAVILION KEY
Isle of Buried Treasure

Marine biology!

GREG LEWBART

Hope you like this story.

Warm regards,

Greg

KRIEGER PUBLISHING COMPANY
MALABAR, FLORIDA
2000

1-17-00

Orlando, FL

Original Edition 2000

Printed and Published by
KRIEGER PUBLISHING COMPANY
1725 KRIEGER DRIVE
MALABAR, FLORIDA 32950

Cover design and map illustration by Susan Stroum

Library of Congress Cataloging-In-Publication Data

Lewbart, Greg.
    Pavilion Key : isle of buried treasure / Greg Lewbart. — Original
ed.
        p. cm.
    ISBN 1-57524-079-3 (alk. paper)
    1. Lepidochelys kempi—Florida—Ten Thousand Islands Fiction.
2. Turtles—Florida—Ten Thousand Islands Fiction. I. Title.
PS3562.E92782P38 1999
813'.54—dc21   99-35645
                                                                        CIP

10 9 8 7 6 5 4 3 2

Dedicated to the memory of Robert James Koller, DVM.

Bob was a devoted father and husband, loyal friend, gifted naturalist, and accomplished clinician who never took a single hour of his life for granted.

Acknowledgments:

I first thank Elaine Harland and the folks at Krieger Publishing for believing in this story and giving it life on the printed page. Sally Young is a gifted copy editor with attention to detail and Floyd Harris helped with the initial outline and first two chapters. I am also grateful to Buck Clark, Julie Mashima, Mr. and Mrs. Krieger, and Dr. Peter C.H. Pritchard for their critical review of the rough draft, and Diane Deresienski, Daniel Lewbart, and Marvin Lewbart for their comments on the final draft.

I thank Howard Krum and Craig Harms for computer assistance, Virginia Whiteford Lewbart, Diane Deresienski, and Michael Ranucci for their on-site Pavilion Key research and in locating crucial library resources. Finally, I acknowledge the love and support provided to me by my wife, Diane, my parents, Marvin and Virginia, and my three brothers, Danny, Randy, and Keith.

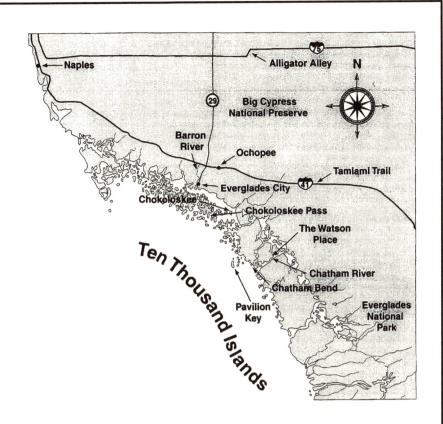

Gulf of Mexico

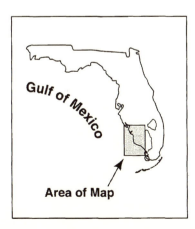

Area of Map

"One of the great mysteries of the sea is the breeding of this turtle. No nests, eggs, pregnant females, or hatchlings have ever been found."

Henry Hill Collins, Jr., *Complete Field Guide to American Wildlife,* 1959

ONE

SIFTING THROUGH JET FUEL-DRENCHED EVERGLADES stew for plane parts and human remains was not what Hal Noble had in mind when he joined the Florida Game and Fresh Water Fish Commission. But then, a lot of what Hal did for a living couldn't be found in any job description.

The recent crash of EcoAir Flight 312 out of Miami put the River of Grass on front pages throughout the world. For almost a month now, news satellites beamed the grim images of rescue workers laden in hip waders working alongside wildlife officers in air boats to every television set in the country. Men and women in throw away surgical masks waded through the swamp, fishing with long hooks for airplane and human parts.

Almost once a day, Hal became angry at how the plane had crashed (cheap parts, shoddy maintenance) and at the futility of the search.

All the passengers were dead.

The blazing late-spring sun was finally sinking, and the search was mercifully called off for another day. Exhausted, filthy, and emotionally drained, Hal just wanted to get to his West Miami hotel room where he could shower, grab a quick dinner, and fall asleep reading a *National Geographic*. He hadn't been able to make it through the first two pages of an intriguing article about the *Titanic* since his arrival.

After a final glance at the grim accident scene, he determinedly walked out of the swamp to get to the airboats carrying the crew back to the main road.

Suddenly, from out of nowhere, a microphone was stuck in his face.

"There have been rumors of alligators attacking rescue workers," came the jarring, midwestern female voice. "Is this true?"

Hal stopped. He looked first at the reporter, Sloan Peebles, who, in sharp contrast to his own disheveled appearance, had every blonde hair in place, and wore an off-white silk blouse and tight-fitting designer jeans under her Miami television station affiliate blazer. Then Hal looked straight at the camera, held by a shaggy-haired college kid in cutoffs.

"No, the alligators have not attacked any rescue workers," Hal replied in an irritated but polite tone.

"How about poisonous snakes?" Sloan persisted, when Hal started to walk off. "Aren't you worried about poisonous snakes? Won't the body parts attract them like they did the gators?"

"Now wait a minute, ma'am," Hal said, stopping again. "These are the facts: When that plane hit the grou. . . . hit the water, going over four hundred miles an hour, you can bet that every gator within a two hundred yard radius was pulverized instantly. And the rest of them have cleared out and won't be back until all of this fuel and hydraulic fluid goes away. Plus, there's just way too much activity here for wild Everglades gators."

"But what about snakes?" Sloan asked.

"As for venomous snakes," Hal emphasized the word venomous—the correct term for animals that inject a toxin, "The only species we see here, deep in the Glades, is the cottonmouth. And they mostly eat fish, which are off swimming with the gators somewhere. They won't have any interest in small body parts."

Hal then snapped one of the swarming mosquitoes out of the air and sandwiched it between the back of his left hand and the palm of his right.

"If you really want to know," Hal nodded to the wide-eyed reporter. "These buggers are the biggest problem we have, next to the heat and humidity." Hal held the back of his tanned and grimy hand near the woman's face.

"Close up on that, Jason," Sloan demanded. "Close up on that."

But before Jason could get Hal's hand in focus, he'd already walked off.

"Okay. Thanks for your help," Sloan called after him. "That was officer Noble. Correct?"

Hal turned around. "Yes. Noble. N-O-B-L-E." Then he picked up the pace to reach the waiting airboat. Over his shoulder he heard Sloan Peebles ordering Jason to the makeshift rescue/recovery camp where a National Transportation Safety Board (NTSB) official was standing drinking some water from a tiny paper cup.

Let them harass that poor bastard for a while, Hal thought. He knew they would edit his interview and cut out the part about how the gators and snakes really weren't a factor. Stuff like this had happened before. They'd air a clip of the interview, introductory material. Then with Hal talking to the reporter they'd mute his conversation and dub in some anchor's voice saying that Officer Noble confirmed that there were gators and poisonous snakes aplenty in these parts and that they posed a big problem (even though this problem was mostly to the fishes and frogs in the swamp). Hal had learned firsthand how sensationalism causes people to act.

There was nothing (otherwise) unusual about the Saturday three weekends ago when the plane went down. Hal and fellow officer Linda Baldwin were easing through their once-a-month weekend duty at the Ochopee Ranger Station at the corner of Route 29 and the Tamiami Trail near Everglades City.

"Big Saturday night plans, Hal?" Linda chirped with a smile, hoping to get a rise out of Hal who she knew almost never went out. She hoped some small talk would prime her nerves enough to fire off a "will you have dinner with me?" volley.

"Nothing too exciting," Hal replied with a shy grin. "I rented a couple of old black and white films that I've been wanting to see. That's about it."

"*Casablanca* stuff?" Linda asked enthusiastically.

"Nah. I'm not much for mushy Bogart stuff? One's an old Cagney flick and the other is an early documentary on shipbuilding."

"Oh," Linda replied softly. *I'd watch a Leggo building contest if he'd only invite me over,* she thought.

Linda was an attractive wildlife officer with shoulder length wavy auburn hair that seemed to jump with life every time she spoke or moved her head. She had a small perfect nose, plump lips, and even white teeth. She kept her thirty-one year old body in good condition and was very likeable although she could be quiet and withdrawn around people she didn't know. She married young, right out of high school, and had been divorced for nearly eleven years. She didn't have any children with her first husband and doubted she'd have any with her second, assuming she acquired a second. The fact that she had a serious crush on Hal was no secret among the other officers, but Hal always pretended he wasn't aware of the situation.

Hal Noble had been a Florida wildlife officer for just over ten years. This job was his life. A bachelor in his mid thirties, Hal could usually be found in his cluttered office doing paperwork or researching a case when he wasn't in the field nabbing poachers. Hal lived in a modest East Naples home and kept fit by going to the gym three or four times per week. His family lived up in the Jacksonville area and he always visited on holidays when he could get away from work.

The Saturday morning had been uneventful. Hal had a couple of minor run-ins with some litterbugs over at a campsite, but that was about it. He and Linda were just finishing the sandwiches he'd picked up at Jane's general store when the phone rang.

"Hal! How the hell are you?" the familiar voice boomed.

Hal had to hold the phone away from his head. "Doing just fine, Roger. What's new with you and the ivory-bill project?"

"Nothin' much," Roger Slocumb said. "Just calling to let you know that all's well with our endangered feathered friends."

Hal could picture Roger. Probably shirtless, long beard still harboring a few flakes of lunch, and those stained red suspenders arcing over his impressive abdomen and straining to keep the blue jeans from falling down around his ankles.

Life hadn't been the same for Hal since the whole ivory-billed woodpecker situation. An unlawful slime of a man named Malcolm Grimes had discovered a pair of ivory-bills, long believed extinct, in the Big Cypress just over a year ago. He sold information on the bird's whereabouts to several interested parties and the chase was on. Hal eventually picked up on the unusual amount of activity in the forest and the whole thing erupted in a heart-pounding confrontation in which Grimes, a Colombian poacher, and a Miami exotic animal dealer named Keith Cutter all died violently. Julie Brooks, an aviary curator, and the Colombian poacher's brother were severely wounded but survived. And Hal was bailed out of a pretty tight situation by Roger Slocumb, a local character with a checkered past and good heart.

Hal was the key figure in the numerous post ivory-bill incident meetings which took place with federal Fish and Wildlife officials, local and state law enforcement officers, and the parties involved in the case. All agreed to make the surviving ivory-bill family the top priority and in a rare display of smothered egos and private agenda dumping, it was decided that the woodpeckers would be left out of all public statements and media interviews. The local papers carried a few stories which lacked specifics about a Big Cypress shootout, the surviving Colombian was quietly deported, the Harvard scientists went back to their grant writing and teaching and agreed to change their research focus, and the aviary-managing Brooks couple sold their

6

house in Kissimmee and moved to the Detroit area where they now owned a Wild Birds Unlimited franchise.

Hal was at ease with the way things turned out. Sure, eventually the story would get leaked and others might even come looking for the birds. But for now, at least, only Slocumb, a few Fish and Wildlife employees, and he knew the exact whereabouts of the ivory-bill nest. Which, by the way, was currently harboring this year's first clutch of eggs.

"Hey. Have you heard about that plane crash near Miami? News of it just came over on my scanner," Roger added.

Hal was surprised. "Plane crash? No. What kind of plane?"

"A big one. At least there's a helluva lot more commotion on the airwaves than there is when one of those Cessna's runs out of fuel in the swamp."

Before Hal could reply, Linda was tugging at his arm and gesturing for him to hang up. She was on the two way radio and looked ashen. A large passenger jet had gone down about fifteen miles west of Miami and they wanted Hal and another field officer to report to the scene immediately. The people running the search and rescue also asked that Hal pack enough stuff for at least a few nights.

That was over three weeks ago, and Hal surveyed the depressing scene from his spot in the large airboat. The curvy reporter was now latched onto the parched NTSB official like a stubborn grass spur. A half dozen jonboats and three airboats plied the stagnant water for pieces. The black boxes and most of the important stuff had been recovered already, and he guessed the search would be called

off in a day or two. The end couldn't come too soon for
Hal. He had never worked a plane crash like this before
and never wanted to work another one. Besides the obvious gory details, this impromptu project had put him behind schedule, and it would take at least a week just to get
caught up on paperwork. It was nearly the middle of June
and his annual reports were all due by the end of the
month.

No. They couldn't end this thing too soon for Hal
Noble.

TWO

THANK GOD THEY FINALLY CALLED THAT THING OFF," HAL muttered to Linda the following Monday as he clicked the front screen door of the Everglades Ranger Station secure behind him.

"Hal!" Linda cried, her hand instinctively rushing up to straighten her hair. "You're back. Are you okay? What was it like? Pretty brutal, huh?"

"I've had more fun," Hal replied. "There's still twenty-five percent of a jetliner and the organic matter of fifty passengers submerged in that baking Everglades muck. But it's time to get back to the standard grind. I'll take poacher nabbing over swamp sifting any day. Any interesting calls?"

"Mostly the usual stuff. I finally caught up with those black bear baiters over near Copeland."

"Well, that's good news," Hal replied as he fixed himself a cup of coffee in the corner of the front office. A small table was set up for that purpose.

Bear baiting is an effective way to hunt black bears. The concept behind the method is basic, even simple. The "hunter" fills up a bucket or barrel with old pieces of meat and fat drippings. This concoction is then left in a secluded area of bear habitat away from human traffic. The unlucky bear or bears find the food and keep coming back as long as the easy fare is available. And the hunter sees to it that the barrel is always full. When bear season opens, the "brave" hunter waits near the supersized bird feeder with rifle aimed and loaded. The bear comes to feed out of hunger and habit and a rug is born. Legal in Maine and a few other states. Very illegal in Florida.

"They'll probably walk with a fine and probation. But a few bears may see another season for it," Linda said as Hal took the first mini sip of his hot coffee. "There is one interesting message here though. It's from Jasper Wiley over at the Rod and Gun Club. Said it wasn't urgent, but that he needed to speak with you when you got back."

"Well, I better not keep the old boy waiting. Probably just another Yankee fisherman keeping an extra redfish or snook," Hal said in an amused but grateful tone. "Maybe even someone doing illegal dumping out off of Route 29."

Jasper Wiley was the seventy-five-year-old desk clerk, bell boy, and part time waiter at the past-its-prime hunting and fishing resort known as the Rod & Gun Club. Jasper moved slowly and deliberately, but he had a lot of stamina for a fellow his age. Thousands of hot sunny days had baked his skin to a deep wrinkled brown. A few strands of gray hair crawled from under his fisherman's cap and a pair of reading glasses swung freely from his leathery neck. He wore loose khaki work pants, an old leather belt with two pronounced buckle holes, and a torn flannel shirt.

The Club, as it was known by the locals, was a subtropical haven for presidents and movie stars in the 1930s and 1940s. The winter climate was unmatched in the continen-

10

tal United States and you had to go to Venezuela to find tarpon fishing that could compare to the waters surrounding the Ten Thousand Islands, just a few pole thrusts of a flat bottom boat from the Club. But over the years the rest of Florida ripened into a tourist mecca with all the amenities and conveniences not found in out of the way Everglades City and its historic Rod & Gun Club.

Jasper was born and grew up in this Florida outpost town and was witness to busier times and famous visitors. It made no difference to him what the economic state of the town was as long as he was there, had food to eat, and a place to live with a good mosquito screen, which he had in the form of his own room at the Club. Jasper had gotten caught up in some of the liquor running and drug smuggling that defined this small town of six hundred or so souls since the 1920s. But he was clean now. Had been for nearly fifteen years. And his favorite pastime was doing detective work for the local Florida Game and Fresh Water Fish officers, of which Hal was his favorite. He had always loved the natural part of his environment, and although he had broken his share of laws, he never stabbed mother nature in the back. Helping out the game warden folks was his way of giving something back.

"Rod and Gun Club, Jasper speakin'," jumped from the receiver of the cordless phone in Hal's hand.

"Jasper, it's Hal from the ranger station. Linda said you called."

"I was wondrin' when you'd get back to me young fella. Where the heck ya been? I left that message three, maybe four days ago."

"Working that plane crash out in the Glades. We've done what we could do so now I'm back on the regular beat," Hal said.

"Yeah. I sorta thought so. Saw on the news where wild-life officers were helpin' out. Much as I like that country, I'm happy stayin' right here. Don't like no kind of crashes, 'specially airplane ones."

"So, what has Inspector Wiley turned up this time?" Hal said in an effort to move the conversation away from the EcoAir crash. He detected a degree of urgency in Jasper's voice.

"Sea turtles," Jasper replied.

"Sea turtles?"

"Yup. We need to talk about sea turtles. But not over the phone. It's too complicated to tell ya right now. Plus I got a lot of folks checkin' in and outta the Club today. It's tarpon season ya know."

"Yes. Right. Tarpon season. Well, when can we have a meeting, inspector?" Hal asked.

"Tomorrow is Saturday and they'll all be out fishin' in the mornin' after breakfast. Why don't we meet over at Smallwood's around ten for an early lunch?" Jasper said with an air of secrecy. "Then we can talk."

"All right. Ten o'clock it is at Smallwoods'."

"Bye Hal."

"G-bye Jasper."

Hal sat for a minute after their conversation had ended, rubbed his right earlobe as he was wont to do when he was deep in thought, and contemplated what Jasper had said. *What about sea turtles had gotten Jasper so wound up?*

THREE

HER LARGE FLAT FLIPPERS PULLED SLOWLY THROUGH the moist sand like oars pushing through stubborn molasses. Turtle number 87-222 was making scientific history. It was just after eleven o'clock on a balmy June Texas night in 1996 and the first Kemp's ridley sea turtle participating in a highly controversial "headstart" program had finally come home to nest. Her eleven-year journey began as a hatchling in a plastic bucket at a laboratory in Galveston, Texas, and included three captures by commercial shrimpers, two nights in a North Carolina fish trap, and a near deadly encounter with a lemon shark that left her with only half a front left flipper. She had beaten overwhelming odds to find this beach. And now she was finally home.

Once she had exceeded the high tide mark, 87-222 began secretly depositing eighty-eight eggs resembling dimpleless golf balls in a hole expertly dug with her back flippers. After the last moist egg tumbled into the sandy chamber, instincts over a hundred million years old instructed the first time mother to carefully cover the nest with sand, pat down the area with her flat undershell or plastron, and begin the long crawl back to the familiarity of the Gulf of Mexico. Before the light of dawn could paint the Padre Island sand, the tenacious female ridley was in the surf with warm salty waves lapping at her carapace. Her first stint at motherhood had been a success.

The Kemp's ridley sea turtle, *Lepidochelys kempi,* is the rarest sea turtle on earth. It is also one of the smallest (only its close Pacific cousin, the olive ridley, is smaller). The largest specimens weigh less than a hundred pounds and their upper shell, or carapace, is frequently as wide as it is long, giving them the appearance of having been pulled from side to side like a piece of thick taffy. Juveniles are dark grey to blackish above, quickly turning white below, while the adults tend to be olive-green on top and yellow to cream underneath. Some captive raised specimens are even mistaken for albinos. Males and females are about the same size, but the males have a longer tail and curved front claws which they use to restrain the female during mating, which always occurs in the water.

No human knows how long ridleys live, or any sea turtle for that matter. They have no rings to count or teeth to analyze. And they haven't been held in captivity long enough to establish captive longevity data. But most of the experts agree that there are plenty of fifty-somethings out there and probably a few octogenarians.

The Kemp's ridley is the seafood connoisseur of the sea turtle family. While the natural diet of the seven species of marine chelonians is influenced by a number of factors including the turtle's age, specific geographic locality, and available food resources, each species does occupy its own culinary niche. The loggerhead is fond of hard shelled invertebrates like clams, conchs, and crabs while the adult green turtle is more of a salad eater, focusing its attention on various seaweeds and algae. The leatherback, giant among the turtle clan, reaches its nearly one ton maximum weight on an insatiable diet of coelenterates (jellyfish, anemones, and comb jellies). And then there's the Kemp's ridley, who would have a field day at a Baltimore crab house. Gut content studies have shown that the adults feed almost exclusively on crustaceans, and in some cases the arthropod of choice happens to be the succulent blue crab. The strong head muscles and powerful beak of the ridley would be way ahead of the best wooden mallet wielder in Maryland if it came to a blue-crab-dispatching race.

The Kemp's ridley was a scientific enigma until the early 1960s. The problem was that no herpetologist knew where they nested. In the early part of this century, most of the natural history information about sea turtles came from scribbled fishing logs and interviews with commercial turtle fisherman. Since the green and loggerhead turtles were economically valuable, it made perfect sense that the fisherman understood their nesting and migration patterns. But the Kemp's ridley was a different story. When boated these feisty turtles went crazy. They would thrash around, injuring the fisherman and themselves, and they wouldn't survive long on their backs, unlike the phlegmatic green. While their small size didn't hurt their market value, they were relatively scarce, so the turtle catchers weren't much help to the scientists when it came to the Kemp's ridley. But one very interesting tidbit continued to surface when the scientists from the north began poking around in the Caribbean for sea turtle information. No one seemed to know where they nested. In fact, very few had ever been seen on a beach! Loggerheads, greens, leatherbacks, and even hawksbills nested on beaches all

over the Caribbean and the southern Atlantic coast of the
United States, but not the ridley. Professional and amateur
herpetologists spent countless nights walking the beaches
of the tropical and subtropical Western Atlantic, surveying
sea turtle nesting sites, and hoping to find some Kemp's
ridleys. But they never found any. This led to a number of
seemingly wild theories about their reproductive strate-
gies. Some thought that they might be a sterile hybrid produced by a mating of the green and loggerhead. This *could*
explain their small size and odd shape, and why they were
never seen nesting. In fact, one of the fishermen's nick-
names for the Kemp's ridley was the bastard turtle—
stemming from their unknown parentage. So the hybrid
theory had at least some merit. But no one had ever seen
greens mate with loggerheads—a problem for the theory.
Another idea was that the Kemp's ridley was simply a dying species that no longer reproduced at all! What was
swimming in the ocean now was all there would ever be of
the ridley. When the last one perished, that would be it.
Bizarre but remotely possible. A few other oddball ideas
on ridley reproduction floated around in the academic sea,
but the famed sea turtle researcher Archie Carr believed in
what was probably the strongest theory: They (the scientists) just hadn't looked hard enough for the nests. Maybe
the turtles were nesting at an odd time of year. Or an odd
time of day. Or both. Surely there were people, native people, who had seen ridleys nest and had consumed fresh
ridley eggs. But finding those people had proved to be
difficult.

Then it happened. In 1961, Professor Henry Hildebrand of Corpus Christi University, who like Carr had also
been pursuing the ridley mystery, finally tracked down a
road construction engineer and private pilot named An-

16

drés Herrera. Hildebrand had been chasing stories and following tips about nesting sea turtles in northern Mexico for several years. His search eventually led him to Herrera, who in June of 1947, had filmed a spectacular scene while flying his small plane over a beach head in northeastern Mexico. Herrera knew that his film was unusual, but not being a biologist, he had simply tucked it away in a drawer for safe keeping. The beach was called Rancho Nuevo and the grainy film showed an estimated forty thousand female Kemp's ridleys crawling along the sand in an effort to dig nests and deposit their species-sustaining ova. The lucky photographer had witnessed and recorded the *Arribada* (the arrival). The riddle of the ridley had been solved and Carr's theory had been the correct one. At Hildebrand's invitation, Carr flew to Mexico from Florida to see the film and confirmed that Herrera's celluloid turtles were indeed nesting ridleys. But the early publicity didn't help the ridley as much as it helped the careers of academic herpetologists, and it took several years for the Mexican government to provide protection for the nests. Although forty thousand might seem like a big number, this represented virtually the entire adult female population of the species. Over the next three decades, pressure from egg poachers, deterioration of the marine environment, and accidental drownings in shrimp trawls reduced the Rancho Nuevo nesting population to about four hundred animals. A critically low number. It was time to do something and the controversial Kemp's Ridley Head Start Experiment was born in 1977.

The Head Start program sounded good on paper. The ridleys' numbers were low and decreasing annually. The remote Mexican beach was difficult to patrol and there were political and legal issues which the biologists were ill equipped to handle. The solution seemed simple enough. Intercept fresh ridley eggs as they fell from the female's vent and place them immediately in sand from a south Texas beach (Padre Island National Seashore). Fly the eggs to the United States. Incubate them under controlled conditions and imprint the new hatchlings for a few seconds in the warm Padre Island waters before recapturing them with white aquarium dip nets. This was termed the "imprinting" portion of the project.

The second part of Operation Head Start involved growing the naturalized hatchlings in yellow five-gallon buckets for between nine and eleven months (their most vulnerable life stage) in a Galveston, Texas "Turtle Barn." The near-yearling turtles were then tagged and released into the sea. Theoretically, they'd swim around for ten or fifteen years, mate, and return to the Texas beach to lay eggs. The result: Instant sea turtle population. But there were a lot of glitches. It took a while to get the husbandry mechanics worked out. Photoperiod and nutrition were problems and many of the early hatchlings had metabolic and bone disorders. Most of the two thousand eggs brought from Mexico to the Galveston laboratory in 1983 were mishandled and rendered infertile.

The imprinting program was eventually discontinued in 1988 since no female Head Start turtles had returned to Padre Island to nest. The entire Head Start program was put on hold in 1992.

In a period spanning roughly fifteen years the Mexican and United States governments spent over four million dollars on the Kemp's ridley project, released over eighteen thousand tagged hatchlings to the wild, and created a lot of controversy and even animosity among biologists, politicians, and bureaucrats. Most of the opponents

18

of the program stressed the importance of focusing funds and other resources on protecting nests, native nesting animals, and enforcing the use of turtle excluder devices (TEDs) on Gulf of Mexico shrimp trawlers. Things eventually got so bad that the biologist who created the program in the 1970s was quoted in 1992 as saying, "I've created a monster."

But then again, *he* didn't know about turtle 87-222.

"Aw crap. Outta frog's legs again," muttered Jasper loud enough for Hal to hear. "And this place has the best damn swamp chicken in the state. *When* they have it, that is."

"If folks would gig 'em, we'd serve him," barked the middle-aged waitress, pulling a pencil from behind her ear and an order pad from her apron. She had overheard Jasper's whining as she approached the table and couldn't let his comments slip by unaddressed.

Jasper looked up at the frowning waitress. "Now Tammy, I didn't mean nothin' by it. Just a man gets a cravin' once in a while that only certain things can satisfy. And for me it's frog's legs. Deep fried and spicy."

Hal sat back, a slight grin on his face, amused by the developing conversation. Smallwood's restaurant on the island town of Chokoloskee was a favorite lunch and breakfast spot for locals. They *did* serve the most delicious frog's legs around and their gator tail was almost as good. But gigging bullfrogs in the middle of a hot south Florida summer night was back-breaking work. The mosquitoes were oppressive, the working conditions grim, and the reward relatively small since there just didn't seem to be as many frogs as there used to be. A lot of folks still went after frogs, but primarily for their own personal consumption.

"Jasper, why not try the grouper? It's probably fresh and they'll cook it how you want it," Hal chimed in.

"Grouper? Here? You know the grouper they serve us natives is nothin' more then spiced up snook. Gimme the chicken salad plate. And a coke," Jasper sighed.

"Make that two, Tammy. But a diet for me," Hal said politely.

Tammy scribbled down their order, adjusted the apron on her stocky but well proportioned frame, and turned toward the kitchen. "I'll be right back with your drinks."

Hal leaned back in his chair. "Now what's all this talk about sea turtles? And why couldn't we just discuss it on the phone?"

"Well, it's like this. Back in the late '40s, just after the war, I was out to Pavilion Key doin' some fishin' in the deep water at the south end of the island one day. Things were goin' real good. I was by myself. Nettin' mullet by the bucket full. The most I'd ever seen. Hell, I was a strong tough bugger back then. So I was doin' everything. Workin' the motor. Droppin' the anchor. Tendin' the nets." Jasper paused, making sure Hal was paying close attention. "Before I know what's what she flips and I'm swimmin'. Lost most of my catch but was able to push the boat to shore. Well, the water wrecked the motor and it wouldn't start. So there I am. Sittin' on the beach at Pavilion Key with a wet boat, empty fish buckets, and a worthless outboard. It was late June. Maybe early July. And there just weren't many folks down here back then. Must've been about two o'clock when I swamped and it was brutal hot. Began to look like I was spendin' the night on old Pavilion. I used the boat to fix me a shelter and decided to stay on the beach where it was breezy. The bugs were much worse

20

inland and the boat kept the sun offa me. I wasn't scared or nothin' 'cause I'd spent the night out in the islands before. A couple a times as' matter of fact." Jasper paused again for effect. "Okay. So here I am, tryin' to nap under the part turned over boat, when I feel somethin' wet and crusty on my leg. And it's movin'! I mean Hal, scared the shit outta me. I jump up, hit my head on the boat seat, and twirl back to the sand. When I look up I'm eye to eye with a damn turtle! One of them old ocean turtles had crawled outta the waves and into my shelter. Well, I knew enough about turtles to know it wouldn't hurt me. And that it was probably only lookin' to make a nest. So I move a little to one side and she keeps on pullin' through the sand til she reaches the dune grass. Then she spends about an hour diggin' a hole. Sand flyin' everywhere. I wasn't so tired any more so I just watched her. And after the hole was to her likin' she squirts a whole bunch of eggs into it, covers it up just so, and crawls back into the Gulf. And she even passes back under my boat! Damndest thing I'd seen in forever."

Hal leaned forward and put his elbows on the small square table. "All quite interesting, Jasper. And a pretty good story. But what's the big deal? The big secret? Sea turtles still nest in the Ten Thousand Islands. Probably even on Pavilion Key."

Jasper started to answer but was stopped short when he noticed the large serving tray that Tammy was expertly balancing just above his left ear.

"Let me know if you need anything else," Tammy said when she had finished putting the plates on the table.

Hal flipped open his paper napkin and sampled one of the greasy french fries. "Looks great."

Jasper looked around the room, leaned over his chicken salad, and began speaking to Hal in a whisper. "I know ocean turtles on the beach is no big thing. But this turtle was no loggerhead, Hal. She was a bastard turtle. You know, a ridley."

Hal stopped chewing, took a big sip of soda, and looked inquisitively at Japser. "A ridley? You mean a Kemp's ridley sea turtle? Nesting on Pavilion Key?"

"That's exactly what I'm sayin'. And that wasn't the end of it. I saw eight more turtles nestin' that day. And who knows how many came the day before. Or the day after? Or the day after that?"

Hal put his Diet Coke down. "Jesus. Are you sure? You sure you know the difference between the loggerhead and the ridley? And the green for that matter."

"I know the diff'rence. Well, I didn't really know when I saw 'em, but I did some readin' at the library and learned somethin' about ocean turtles. These Pavilion egg layin' turtles weren't much bigger than an old Everglades snapper. Them other turtles, greens and loggerheads I mean, are at least twice that big when they're carryin' eggs. Then I did some more readin' and found some newer articles tellin' about biologists discovering the mystery nestin' beach of the Kemp's ridley turtle in Mexico. And the thing that really caught my eye was these articles sayin' that Kemp's ridleys didn't nest nowhere else in the world! And I found em right here on Pavilion!"

"How come you never told me this before?" Hal asked with surprise.

"C'mon Hal, there's lots of crap I haven't told 'ya. Not on purpose now. I just keep some things to myself. And this ridley turtle thing was one of my big secrets."

Hal was sure this is where things would get interesting. "So why tell me now? Why ruin your secret?"

"Well. I've been checkin' on these Pavilion ridleys over

the years. Not every season, mind 'ya. No time for that. But when I wasn't too busy in June or July I'd head over to Pavilion to see the turtles. And they always came. Some days two or three. Some days more. Fourteen was the most I ever saw in a day."

"Yeah," Hal said slowly, trying to lead Jasper to the point. "You're still not telling me what's changed."

"Hal. I think the Pavilion ridleys are in danger. Can we take a ride out there in your Whaler? I'll tell you everythin' on the way."

FOUR

Okay. Let's see the rest of the stuff," Dean Applegate said to the two men standing beside him.

The smaller of the two nodded lazily to the other, who was wearing old jeans, a torn long sleeve flannel shirt with the sleeves rolled up, and a worn baseball cap. The large man moved slowly across the small, primitive room and grabbed hold of two large burlap sacks, the kind used to hold onions or potatoes. Both were tied tightly at their tops with course twine giving them the impression of having pinched hairdos. He lifted the sacks easily and carried them to the small man.

"Is this everything?" Applegate asked quickly. A nervous edge to his voice.

"All we got," the small man, whose name was Bass, replied. Whitcomb Bass was in his early forties, had a thin strip of hair resembling a squirrel's tail at the top of his head, and was about forty pounds overweight. He moved with some effort and stepped back as the uniformed U.S. Fish and Wildlife officer began untying the first sack.

"One . . . two . . . three . . . fourrrr. . . . five," Applegate whispered to no one in particular as he shifted the bag from side to side. He did the same with the second. But counted to six.

"That's fifteen pygmy rattlers, twenty-two kings, and the eleven indigos," Applegate said as he retied the heavy bags. "Make it an even thousand."

Bass nodded to the larger man who pulled a chained biker's wallet from his pocket, unclipped it, and handed it to Bass. As Applegate watched intently, Bass licked his right thumb and forefinger several times as he counted out ten one hundred dollar bills and handed them to Applegate.

Applegate held the money tightly, gazed at it for what seemed an unnecessary moment, folded the bills in half, and slid them into his right front pants pocket. Then he turned and left the single-roomed hunting camp. No good-byes were exchanged.

This was a fairly typical encounter for Derrick "Dean" Applegate. A number of poachers used this and other Big Cypress hunting camps like it as a place to do business with Applegate. Superficially, Applegate was the perfect wild-life officer. Eighteen flawless years of service. A couple of commendations. Got along well with coworkers. And he had a loving, well-balanced family. Applegate was forty-two years old, kept himself in good physical shape, had one of those distinguished handsome faces produced by a square jaw, strong even nose, eyes so brown they looked black, and graying temples that faded to a full crop of dusty brown hair. His uniforms looked like they were pressed twice a day and even his patrol Ford Bronco was spotless most of the time. His nickname at work was "poster boy." And for helping out a couple of reptile poach-ers, poster boy was a thousand dollars richer.

The first time was the hardest. No question. And now Applegate was addicted to money like a druggie to the little white rocks. It had happened eleven years ago. Applegate, who had sworn to himself after he cheated on the U.S. Fish and Wildlife entrance exam that he'd never do anything shady again, had just caught a guy near Fakahatchee Strand with three Florida indigo snakes. A threatened species with federal protection, these beautiful snakes have huge dark scales like an old slate roof. Only the largest timber rattler rivals them in size. The poacher took a big chance and offered Applegate five hundred dollars to let him go. At first Applegate was beside himself with anger and disgust. Then the thought of what five hundred dollars could do began to swallow his thinking. Hell, that was more money then he made in a whole week! Plus he was overworked. Had a new baby, and a wife with an insatiable shopping habit. Shit, the five hundred could cover the mortgage and then some. And who would know? Who would care?

The poacher had started to pocket the bribe when he saw Applegate's initial reaction, then watched as Applegate's anger metamorphosed into a serious but nervous state.

Applegate had taken the money and hasn't stopped since. He maintained some control of his habit by following two rules. He only worked with a handful of "customers" and never did the bribes exceed his salary. These limits had served him well. He'd never been caught. And he planned to quit taking bribes at the end of the year when the new home on Marco Island was finished.

Applegate knew that most of the poachers he dealt with were taking more than they showed him, but by inspecting them regularly, he was able to keep the cash flowing like a deeply drilled well.

FIVE

SCATTERED LIKE WILD FLOWERS IN A FIELD, AND JUST AS indistinguishable, the rich mangrove islands that comprise Florida Bay's Ten Thousand Islands make up an ecosystem unique to North America. Green, hot, and virtually impenetrable, these islands hang from the edge of the Everglades like an emerald necklace. They lie in tannin-stained water that ranges from slightly brackish to completely saline. The countless watery pathways that keep the islands from congealing into a single land mass range in depth from a few inches to several feet. All depending on the tide, of course. These islands are like living beings since mangrove trees have the ability to slowly "walk" by expanding their branches and root system across shallow water to visit neighboring plants. Thus, two small islands can become one in a matter of several years. The dynamic nature of the islands, and the fact that they all look alike, pose real problems for anyone trying to navigate these waters. There are only three or four marked channels in the entire Ten Thousand Islands.

Experienced fishing guides have their private landmarks and flat bottomed boats that draw less than six inches of water. But even they get nervous if they make a wrong turn or follow a large snook chasing bait into an unknown cove. Many lost and stranded mariners have spent sleepless nights swatting mosquitoes and anxiously counting the hours until dawn in the Ten Thousand Islands.

Pavilion Key is a member of the Ten Thousand Islands. But Pavilion Key is not one of those start-up mangrove islets born from a lone floating pod that happens upon just enough dirt and oyster shell to support a single arc-rooted tree. It is a true island with a real sandy beach and deep water separating it from its neighbors. There are even a few native palm trees scattered about the dense vegetative veneer covering it's nearly half a mile long and an eighth of a mile wide body. Pavilion Key is also the farthest out to sea of the Ten Thousand Islands.

There are currently no man-made structures on Pavilion Key, save for a Port-A-Potty tended to by the Everglades National Park Service. Adventurous folks like to paddle out to Pavilion Key and camp there, especially in the winter when the mosquitoes have died back a bit. But this isn't to say that there were never structures on Pavilion Key. In the early part of the twentieth century plume hunters and island farmers tried to tame Pavilion Key. But no one stayed very long. The lack of fresh potable water was the island's most effective weapon against human invaders.

Several hundred years ago Pavilion Key was a busy place, surely with more human activity than it has now. Before the white man killed off the last Calusa Indian about 1750, Pavilion Key was a place where the Calusa gathered turtle eggs, hunted small game, and camped on extended fishing trips. They may have even had semi-

permanent camps on the island. Caribbean pirates fre-
quented the island in the seventeenth, eighteenth, and
early nineteenth centuries because it was out of the way
and had a small deep bay on its southeast side where larger
wooden ships could anchor safely. It was some of this pirate activity that gave Pavilion Key its name.

The year was 1818 and a particularly successful and
ruthless American-born pirate named Charles Gibbs had
just captured and pillaged a Dutch bark carrying West Indian produce and silver. Gibbs and his murderous crew
had been crisscrossing the Caribbean for some time in the
privateer *Maria*, a ship Gibbs and his cohorts had taken by
mutiny from the appointed captain and officers. The
Gibbs crew had taken an oath to kill all those aboard any
ship they captured in an effort to eliminate eye-witness accounts of their terrible deeds. They had already taken Brit-
ish, French, and American ships when they came upon the
Dutch vessel. Gibbs and his evil bullies had brutally murdered every sailor up until then and planned the same fate
for the Dutch crew. And, indeed, they did snuff out the life
of each begging Dutchman, one by one, until all thirty had
been killed and tossed to the waiting sharks below. It was a
savage sight, and witnessed by a golden-haired, seventeen-
year-old virgin named Kaaren Van Bokkelen. The pirates
had saved the girl for last, and when it was her turn to die,
she threw herself at Gibbs's feet and begged the twenty-
four-year old buccaneer for mercy. Motivated by lust
alone, Gibbs spared the girl and retained her as his captive
love interest. But a woman on a sailing ship was bad luck in
the early 1800s, and Gibbs's crew began to put pressure on
him to kill the girl. Plus, they insisted, she was a witness to
their crimes and could get them all hanged if she survived.
Gibbs persisted in keeping the girl alive and even brought

her to the crew's island hideout just southeast of Cape Romano in the Florida Bay. Here, he built a small wooden structure for the girl, to protect her from the south Florida elements. He would visit her on a daily basis while his men stayed on board ship. Protecting her became more difficult as the days wore on and he even had to shoot one of his men who made an attempt to beat Kaaren to death with a club. When the pirate crew threatened Gibbs with mutiny if he didn't let them kill the girl, Gibbs backed down and volunteered to do the deed himself. But Gibbs, as terrible as he was, couldn't summon up the will to dispatch her with hot lead or cold blade. So he had the cook brew a poisonous stew and she died a slow, retching death under the wooden pavilion Gibbs had constructed to shelter her. The *Maria* cast off soon after Gibbs buried young Kaaren Van Bokkelen.

Several days later the United States schooner *Porpoise,* in search of pirates in the area, discovered the dead girl's shallow grave next to the unusual wooden structure. Lieutenant James Ramage, the commander of the *Porpoise,* wrote the name Pavilion Key next to the long sandy-shored island on his charts. It's been known as Pavilion Key ever since.

Gibbs and his band of murderers accidentally wrecked the *Maria* a few weeks later and had to destroy her on the beach. After procuring a stolen brigantine from the famed pirate Gasparilla, via Gibbs' agent in Havana, Gibbs poisoned the Caribbean for another four years before narrowly escaping from a losing skirmish with some United States Marines. He spent the next eighteen months working as a semi-legitimate sailor on ships between Havana, Liverpool, New Orleans, and Philadelphia. But the pirating soul would not wash from Gibbs, and in the spring of

30

1823, he was captured in New York after committing a particularly ruthless murder and hanged by the neck until dead.

"I guess it was 'bout three days ago. Must've been 'cause it was Sunday. I was anchored off of Little Pavilion fishin' for trout and had to take a dump," Jasper said as he unfastened the safety strap that secured Hal's Game and Fish boat to its trailer.

"Were you alone?" Hal asked as he tightened down the drain plug in the stern of the twenty-one foot Boston Whaler.

"Was I alone? C'mon Hal, you know I only fish by myself. Fishin' is my private time. . . . the only chance for a man to find a little peace. So anyway, I scoot over to Pavilion to use that Port-O-John. Real toilet paper ya know. And I see some footprints and a stick long enough to get into a turtle's nest not far from where I beach my skiff."

"There must be a thousand sticks on that island." Hal said, unimpressed.

"But them footprints. In the middle of summer. Now that's gotta be somethin'," Jasper replied.

"You might be right. It's certainly worth a look see," Hal said getting back into his Chevy Blazer and flipping it into reverse. Jasper grabbed the bow line and walked slowly to the wooden dock. Hal expertly backed the Blazer down the submerged cement ramp and the Whaler slid off of the trailer like a package from a conveyer belt. Jasper secured the boat to a pier cleat while Hal parked the truck and trailer.

Hal climbed into the boat and primed the Johnson 135 horsepower outboard. "You said *some* footprints. Could you tell if there was more than one person?"

"Yeah. One guy. And I'll tell ya how I know. These were big prints. Made by boots. And they all looked exactly the same. This was no retired person's shell collecting trip," Jasper said as he followed the freed bow and stern lines into the Whaler.

Hal put the engine in reverse and they turned and began to pull away from the Chokoloskee Marina at idle speed. It was still easy to talk above the quiet outboard.

"Maybe he was another fisherman in need of a toilet?" Hal said skeptically.

"Yeah, maybe. But the prints were concentrated in an area where I've seen ridley's nestin'. And this spot was a good hundred yards out of the way from the toilet."

"Well it can't hurt to check it out," Hal said. "It's gonna be calm on the Gulf today. Nothing like a fast flat ride out to Pavilion on a hot afternoon."

Hal continued to idle the Whaler around Chokoloskee until he reached Sand Fly Pass where he opened up the Johnson outboard, spooking a great blue heron that was picking off bait fish amidst the nearby mangroves. The spinning stainless steel prop churned up the murky water like a blender making a milkshake, and soon Hal and Jasper were skimming past the last small islands and into the Gulf of Mexico. Hal noted to himself that each red and green channel marker along the way was crowned with an osprey nest, a sight unheard of twenty years ago. At least one species was winning the extinction battle, he thought.

Once they were in the Gulf, Hal headed southeast, and they could soon see Pavilion Key five miles in the distance. Just a glimmering green smudge at first, but in ten minutes the smudge grew to be an island and a few minutes later the white sandy rim that was the beach came into view. They skirted Little Pavilion Key with its shallow dendritic oyster bars and closed in on Pavilion. As they passed Little Pavilion, Hal wondered how the brown pelicans, which spiraled from the sky and into the warm brine after fish, never ended up skewering one of those oyster bars or coming up with an empty pouch.

Hal edged the Whaler up to the shore and Jasper jumped from the bow and onto the hot sand. Hal had picked a good spot with some deep water close to the beach. Jasper didn't even get his feet wet.

"Nice job," Jasper said as he tied the bow line to a half buried driftwood tree stump.

Hal joined Jasper on the sand and they started walking at a good pace to the south. The Port-O-John was about a hundred feet north of their landing site.

The beaches on Pavilion Key are wide, thirty to fifty feet in most places, and covered with mollusc and crustacean shells. Adding diversity to the population of colorful shells are pieces of driftwood, mangrove rhizoids, the occasional beer or soda can, crab trap line, fishing buoys, hunks of styrofoam, dried up seaweed, and a few coconuts. As the beach turns into island, prickly pears give way to sharp grasses, palmettos, sable palms, and a few ironwoods and gumbo limbo trees. Once away from the beach the foliage is jungle thick and nearly impossible to walk through.

"Why would someone come all the way out to Pavilion and dig for turtle eggs?" Jasper said as they closed in on the foot print spot.

"Black market I guess. Cakes and pies. All that stuff. But I'm sure a regular old chicken egg does as good a job as a sea turtle's," Hal said. "But you're right. Why come to Pavilion? Sure it's out of the way. But how many nests could there be here? Not enough to make it worthwhile."

Just then Jasper pointed ahead to a scuffed up area

of sand just above the high tide mark. The footprints were no longer sharp and clear but they were distinguishable. Rounded depressions in the soft sand. Probably made by boots as Jasper had guessed. And there was a long stick among the anonymous prints. About four feet in length. Sturdy and smooth.

Hal picked up the nearly straight pole. "This is no piece of driftwood. Looks to be from a hardwood. Maple or oak."

"Meanin' that the guy *brought* the stick here?" Jasper said.

"That's what I'm thinking. But why wouldn't he just take it back with him?" Hal said. "Unless he didn't want to take the chance of being caught with it."

"Could be. Anyways, take a look over here," Jasper said as he pointed to a spot in the sand about eight feet away and close to some prickly pear plants.

Hal looked to where Jasper was pointing and noticed a small circle of moon snails, neatly seated in the sand with their tops poking out like freshly planted tulip bulbs. The shell circle was about ten inches in diameter.

"Nest marker," Hal said. "Gotta be."

"Yeah. Just what I was thinkin'. And look, there's another right over there," Jasper said, indicating a spot about fifteen feet away to the south using the nest stick he had taken from Hal as a pointer.

The other marker was almost identical to the first. A near perfect ring of walnut sized moon snail shells.

"So our guy has done some poking around and marked a couple of nests. Let's see if we can find anymore." Hal said.

Hal and Jasper spent the next twenty minutes walking the beach, turning up one other shell ring.

"Where else do the ridley's nest on the island?" Hal asked.

"Only on the western shore, and mostly in this area. Far as I know," Jasper replied.

"Okay. Three marked nests here," Hal said. "But there could be more anywhere along this side of the island. That what you're saying?"

"Yup. I've seen 'em crawl ashore all along this side. 'Cept near the points of the island," Jasper said.

"So here's the puzzler. If this guy is hunting turtle eggs for the black market—for baking or whatever—why not just dig the damn eggs up and sell them? They won't be any good once they've got little turtle embryos inside sucking up all that yolk," Hal said.

"Dunno. Maybe he's waitin' 'til he can find a bunch of nests, dig 'em all up at once, and sell the lot as a one time deal," Jasper replied.

"Still. Digging up sea turtle nests is hard, back-breaking work, especially for one person. If it were me, I'd dig them up as I found them and maybe store the eggs somewhere until I had a bunch to sell," Hal said.

"Good point. But what the hell, Hal. We're just guessin' at what's goin' on here. I think we need to do a little more investigatin'."

Hal shook some sand from the tops of his boots. "Okay. An investigation it is. I'm counting on you for help since I can't be zipping out here to Pavilion every day or two. There's too much going on back at the station and in Big Cypress these days. Let's head back and work out the details later."

Jasper shook his shoes too. "Count me in. I can come out this way every day if ya need me to. 'Cept Saturdays of course when we're real busy at the Club. But I can come early on Sunday mornings. No church for me, ya know."

Hal and Jasper walked back to their landing site, shoved the Whaler easily back into the warm Gulf waters, higher now with the rising tide, and motored toward Chokoloskee.

They didn't talk much on the ride back, choosing instead to be alone with their thoughts which held fast in their heads in spite of the forced warm air that flattened their cheeks, watered their eyes, and spun their hair into soft, salty knots.

SIX

Give that to me again! Sea turtles?" WINSLOW
Greene, the owner of Dade Reptiles and Exotics, shouted
into the phone. "Did you say goddamn baby sea turtles?"

"Yes, Winslow. Baby sea turtles. Kemp's *ridley* sea turtles," the male voice on the other end of the line said. It
belonged to Dean Applegate.

"Well, shit Dean. I dunno. I've gotten lots of stuff for
people. Big critters, little critters. Venomous, endangered,
you name it. But never no damn sea turtles." Winslow exhaled a cloud of cigarette smoke through his urine-colored
teeth. "You sure there's a market?"

"Yeah. There's a market. You think I would waste your
time if there wasn't? And *please* don't use my real name
over the phone. Remember?"

"Aw crap. Yeah, I remember. The line might be
tapped," Winslow chuckled, his huge belly rising and falling in a game of hide-and-seek with his belt. Greene was
forty-seven years old, weighed nearly three hundred
pounds, showered once, maybe twice a week, and chain-
smoked Pall Malls. A few strands of gray greasy hair picked

their way across his large scalp, and he had a black and white scruffy beard which was really no more than a week's worth of not shaving. "So what kind of market you talkin' about?"

Applegate was quick to answer. "Well, I checked with a couple of my contacts here and there and they said there's some Europeans and Asians looking for young sea turtles to keep in captivity."

Greene was confused. "You mean zoos? Aquariums?"

"No. Pets! I'm talking about as pets in people's homes. Rich people. Like those folks with nothing better to do with their money than spend it on twenty thousand dollar reef systems and koi ponds," Applegate said.

Greene was silent for a moment. He tapped at an old coffee mug with his pencil and soon began doodling on some paper at his desk. "The ridley's the endangered one, right?"

"That's the one. Rarest sea turtle in the world. And the smallest too," Applegate said.

"How small is small?" Greene asked. He was pretty current on his herp natural history and was busy trying to dredge up sea turtle facts from that part of his brain where he stored such information. But most of that space had been reserved for terrestrial and freshwater aquatic species. He had no need for things he couldn't sell.

"A big adult weighs about eighty pounds. Plenty of 'em in the fifty to sixty pound range. And the hatchlings. . . . well. . . . they're little of course. I'm sure you've seen pictures," Applegate said excitedly, happy that he seemed to be getting Greene's attention.

"Yeah, I know what baby sea turtles look like," Greene said. "Seen the nature shows. The nest opens and it's a moving seafood buffet for any predator in the area. I always liked it when a big old crab would carry one of the little buggers off. Sort of like, 'you're parents might eat me, but I can eat you.' Now that was some good TV."

"Well, from what I can tell, that crab might have been eating a pretty expensive dinner. I'm talking big bucks," Applegate said.

"What's big bucks to you, Dean. . . . shit. . . . sorry. What's big bucks to you, *Larry*?" Greene said, trying not to snicker.

Applegate was not amused but ignored Greene's use of his name again. "Ten thousand dollars. How does ten thousand dollars per hatchling sound?"

"Sounds all right," Greene said calmly. "Real good, actually. How many you think the market could take?"

"My guess is . . . and it's just a guess . . . fifty to a hundred. And that's Europe and Asia. We could probably dump a few here in the U.S. too. But I wouldn't want to flood the market. Keep the demand high," Applegate said.

"Don't you mean *we* wouldn't want to flood the market. I'm assuming you're calling me to help you get rid of these things," Greene said sharply.

"Of course. Of course it's we."

"You're talking as if you've *got* these baby turtles. Now I don't pretend to know as much about sea turtles as I do about other herps, but isn't the ridley the one that only nests on some out of the way beach in Mexico?"

"That's the one. Rancho Nuevo is the name of the place. And believe it or not, I've found my own mini Rancho Nuevo right here in Florida!"

"So you think you could get fifty hatchlings with no trouble?" Greene asked, seemingly unimpressed with the magnitude of Dean's discovery.

"Are you kidding?" Applegate blurted with confidence. "I could get that many from one nest! And since I know where the nesting beach is, this thing could be our own little golden goose. A nice half million or so every year. Assuming the market would support it."

"A half million gross. What kind of a split did you have in mind?" Greene said.

"I was thinking fifty-fifty. Right down the middle. I would supply you with the live hatchlings and you would make sure they got to where they needed to go. And collect the money too, of course," Applegate said.

"Of course. But it seems like I'd be the one taking the risk. Getting caught peddling endangered ridley sea turtles would pretty much finish me. Sixty-forty," Greene said firmly.

Applegate had anticipated something like this, and frankly, would have been content with twenty-five percent if it came to that.

"Okay. Sixty-forty it is. But don't forget I'm taking some risks too."

"Yeah right. You might get caught and lose your cushy fed job," Green replied sarcastically.

"Hey. You know there's nothing cushy about my job. I bust my ass running around these swamps trying to keep my boss and my family happy," Dean said defensively.

"Okay. Whatever. But I don't feel sorry for you. And trust me. I'll be earning my sixty percent. Assuming your info on a market is right. And that you can come up with these rare turtles."

"Don't worry about the market or the turtles. I'll take care of my end of this thing. Just be ready to do your stuff when I call," Applegate said.

"Okay. You know where I'll be," Greene said, and hung up the phone.

Applegate held the receiver in his hand, deep in thought, until the obnoxious "off the hook" beeping tone startled him. As he replaced the receiver, he second guessed his choice of Winslow Greene, but reassured himself with the knowledge that of all the shady pet dealers he knew in Miami, Greene was the most trustworthy.

About the time Applegate and Greene were having their phone conversation, Hal was at the Ranger station office sorting through some paperwork when Linda approached.

"Well, *you* sure look busy. Still doing plane crash stuff?" Linda asked as she leaned just a little lower than necessary over the desk in front of Hal. Her hair was perfect, he thought. She was wearing just enough light makeup. She smelled great. And gravity was drawing her breasts toward him like ripe citrus waiting to be picked.

"Ah . . . No. Finished with the EcoAir thing. I'm busy with another project. Out in the Ten Thousand Islands. Something old Jasper from the Rod and Gun Club has cooked up for me," Hal said, lightly flustered by Linda's appearance but trying to remain composed.

"Sounds interesting. How 'bout dinner tonight? My place. I'll cook and you can tell me all about it," Linda said, certain that Hal couldn't elude her this time.

"Oh. . . . well. . . . tonight's not really good for me," Hal said meekly. "I'm working late, then going to the gym. Maybe some night next week?"

"Next week? It's only Tuesday. What about tomorrow?" Linda persisted. "Are you working out tomorrow *too?*"

Hal knew he was trapped. He wasn't going to be able to wriggle out of this dinner thing. It wasn't that he didn't *want* to have dinner with Linda. Some day at least. Or that he didn't like her, because he did. In fact he was very attracted to her. He just wasn't ready for a relationship. And he didn't know when he would be. *Damn you Alison,* he thought.

Alison Carver and Hal had lived together for almost five years. They met at a softball game in Naples almost seven summers ago. Hal played for one team and Alison for another. Hal was a short stop and had to tag Alison out in a run down one night. He tried to touch her as softly as possible with his glove, but his momentum and the large ball that filled the webbing made a light thump on her back when he tagged her out. The inning ended before he could say anything, so after the game he caught up with her in the parking lot and apologized.

"Don't be silly. It didn't hurt at all," Alison said with a laugh. "I was the dummy that should have stayed on second."

"Well, I still feel bad. I wasn't expecting you to stop so suddenly," Hal said, relieved that she wasn't mad at him.

"Alison Carver. And you are?"

"Hal. Hal Noble."

"Well it's nice to meet you, Hal," Alison said as she snapped the dirt out of her softball cleats. She was sitting on the tailgate of her small pickup with her feet and legs dangling below her. Dirt smudged her uniform here and there and a plump ponytail of strawberry blonde hair poked through the space between the cloth of her hat and the adjustable plastic strap. She had about ten well placed freckles on her face, a small nose which was turned up ever so slightly, lips like curled rose petals, and blue-green eyes that reminded Hal of the Florida sky just before a big thunderstorm.

"I'm glad to meet you too," Hal said smiling. "I guess I'll see you around."

Hal looked her up in the phone book and called the next day since he didn't see a ring on her finger. He left a message on her answering machine and she called back that night. A lunch date led to dinner and a movie and within three months they were serious. A year later they got a place together. Neither of them were ready for marriage so they simply cohabitated and enjoyed their lives together. They eventually joined the same softball team, spent weekends traveling throughout the state, and in the winter they would always pick a different place to go skiing.

Alison was a high school social studies teacher and she took night courses towards a master's degree at Gulf Coast University near Fort Myers. Hal was very supportive of her academic pursuits and was even willing to move if the master's opened the door to a better job opportunity somewhere else. Hal was sure they would get married one day . . . it was just a matter of time. But it never came to that.

Hal and a couple of his Game and Fish buddies had planned a three day canoe camping trip in the Ten Thousand Islands one November weekend. Hal had spent several hours packing and planning the trip. Alison had even helped him get ready. His friends picked him up at home early on Saturday morning and he kissed Alison goodbye, telling her he would see her Monday night.

Alison gave him the mandatory "be careful" and "have a good time" spiel as he walked out the door.

Hal and his friends started their trip uneventfully. Hal and a guy named Reid were in one canoe and the other fellow, named Mark, along with most of their supplies, were in the other. They had put in at Everglades and were about two hours into their trip when Mark unexpectedly capsized. To this day no one is sure how it happened. Just a freaky weight shift perhaps. A lot of the stuff wasn't secured to the boat and most of their supplies were lost. So they righted the overturned canoe and paddled home. They all agreed to try the trip again in a few weeks.

Hal decided that he would surprise Alison and elected not to call her with the news of the aborted trip. He even stopped on his way home and picked up some flowers, and since it was nearly lunch time, he grabbed a pizza with her favorite toppings too.

He tried to be extra quiet as he approached the house in order to maximize the surprise factor. He softly opened the front door, entered the living room area, and was just in time to see the naked buttocks of a man as he finished the down stroke atop Alison who was sprawled face up on the carpeted living room floor. She was moaning with pleasure until she heard the pizza and flowers hit the floor as they dropped from Hal's hands. For a few seconds nothing happened. Only the back of the naked man moved as he tried to catch his breath. He never even turned his head. Alison's wide eyes looked first at the pizza box, then at the flowers, and finally up to Hal's face which appeared pale and lifeless. Like a statue, really. "Oh, God," she muttered softly.

Shock, anger, rage, but most of all surprise filled Hal's heart. He stared at the scene before him for what seemed like five minutes but in reality was closer to five seconds. Then he turned, walked through the still open doorway, and never saw Alison Carver again.

"No. I'm not working out tomorrow. I never go to the gym two days in a row," Hal said.

"Well it's settled then," Linda said smiling. "Dinner at my place tomorrow night. How does seven sound?"

"Okay. Seven sounds good. What can I bring?" Hal asked softly.

"Well, I was thinking about making pizza. So maybe some nice red wine. You like pizza, don't you?"

"Yeah. Sure. Pizza sounds great."

SEVEN

"DAMMIT! WHERE THE HELL ARE THOSE BUCKETS?" Applegate said out loud as he rummaged through the cluttered garage, tossing aside a tricycle and some mud-caked garden tools. "Sooz!" he yelled towards the open door leading to the laundry room of the house. After hearing no answer, he shouted again, "Sooz. . . . aaan! Have you seen my doughnut buckets?"

"Did you say something, honey?" Susan Applegate replied as she skipped down the stairs towards the garage. What was he yelling about this time, she wondered.

"I said, have you seen my doughnut buckets?" Applegate was still yelling, even though he could plainly see that his wife was now standing in the doorway to the garage. Her husband's loud words didn't seem to phase her and she calmly replied, "You mean the white ones? The fishing pails?"

"Yes. Of course the white ones. Do I have any *other* doughnut buckets?"

"They're where you left them last," she said. "Stacked out back in the tool shed."

"Christ, I've spent the past twenty minutes searching for those things. Nothing is ever where you need it
around this damn place," Applegate said as he stomped
past her on his way to the backyard where the small tool
shed was.

Susan was left standing in the doorway, her sandy
blonde hair hanging in thin shiny strands around her face
and down to her shoulders. She was in good shape for
forty-two, tall and thin, with tan skin and a decent complex-
ion. If it weren't for the crow's feet around her eyes she
could have easily passed for ten years younger. She and
Dean had been married for fifteen years so she was used to
his little tirades. But he seemed unusually edgy these past
few days.

Dean quickly found the white five gallon buckets he
had been searching for. Six or seven of them were stacked
neatly in a corner of the shed. Two still had their partially
peeled labels: Raspberry Jelly and Creamy Eclair.

Applegate had done his homework with regard to
hatching sea turtles. There was plenty of accurate data in
the scientific literature on the subject and the National Marine Fisheries Service (NMFS) had recently published a
complete review of the controversial Kemp's ridley head
start program. This document was particularly valuable
for Applegate since it described in cookbook fashion how
to remove eggs from a nest, set them up in sand-filled five
gallon buckets, and properly regulate temperature and humidity in order to produce a high percentage hatch. The
only thing left to do was get back out to Pavilion Key, dig up
the eggs, and set them up in the security of his garage.

"Going fishing?" Susan asked Dean who was now rins-
ing out four of the buckets with a garden hose.

"Fishing? Yeah, I'm going fishing. The redfish are

pretty thick out by Chatham Bend these days. Thought I'd bring one home for dinner tonight."

"Who you going with?" Susan asked.

"Oh. No one. Decided to fish by myself today. Need a little peace and quiet."

Odd, Susan thought. He almost always went fishing with a couple of his buddies. Either the guys from Fish and Wildlife or some of his friends he played tennis with.

"Well, I'm not busy today," Susan said optimistically. "Maybe I could go along. Pack us a nice lunch and we could stop at the old Watson place and have a picnic. Remember, the kids are off with the Hollingtons today." The Hollingtons lived around the corner and the Applegate and Hollington kids were nearly inseparable.

"God, Sooz. I don't know. The skeeters are pretty brutal out at Watson's this time of year. Can't you find something to keep yourself occupied with here at home? The garage is a mess, for one thing."

Another failed effort at quality time, Susan thought. The time she and Dean spent alone together, even just to talk, had been on a steady decline for the past few years. And like a runaway truck on a mountain road, things were getting progressively worse.

Susan Applegate was something of a history buff. And like a ravenous female mosquito, she had consumed everything she could find in the Naples Public Library on the history of the Big Cypress Swamp, the Everglades, and the Ten Thousand Islands. Her absolute favorite story of all was that of Mr. Watson, a turn of the century drifter who like many outlaws and ne'er-do-wells in the 1890s, had percolated through the state of Florida before settling in the wild fringe town of Chokoloskee. But even the end-of-the-earth Chokoloskee was too crowded for Watson, who with the help of one of the first combustion powered boats in the region, built his own small banana and sugar cane plantation on the Chatham river about ten miles southeast of Chokoloskee. To get to the Chatham river, you first had to enter Chatham Bend, a small shallow bay that funneled mariners safely through a myriad of anonymous islands into the river. The Watson place, as the locals referred to it, was on an area of high ground at the western bank of the Chatham where there was deep water access and a good view both up and down river. Watson sold his produce to growing markets in Key West and Tampa. Despite the slow but steady population increase in southern Florida, only two hundred white people lived between Key West and Fort Myers in 1895, an area of coastline stretching nearly two hundred and fifty miles.

Things didn't end up so well for Mr. Watson however. A couple of dead bodies turned up near Chatham Bend one day and at least two other people who worked for Watson mysteriously disappeared. Rumors and mild panic spread through Chokoloskee, and one fall day as Watson sputtered into town to buy supplies, some of the local renegades were waiting for him at the boat landing. They hadn't actually planned to kill Watson, just run him out of the area, but when sweaty fingers touch loaded guns, bad things happen. The historical accounts vary as to who fired first, but once the shooting began, there wasn't much left of Ed Watson. He never even had time to draw his own loaded weapon.

Folks lived on at the Watson place into the 1950s, but after the Park Service took things over, the buildings weren't maintained and were eventually torn down. All that remained of the old plantation was the cement cistern and some crumbling foundations. But there was a picnic table, a place to tie your boat, and a portable outhouse. And best of all, Susan thought, you could spend a few hours there and never see or hear another human soul.

"Okay. You win. Go fish or whatever you have to do. But maybe one of these days we could do *something* together," Susan said, resignation in her voice. "We are actually married to each other."

"We will. We will. I promise. I just need to be alone today, that's all," Applegate said, somewhat relieved that he wouldn't have to further explain himself.

He finished packing up his buckets and other supplies and threw everything into his pickup. Then he backed up to the boat trailer with its attached nineteen foot Carolina Skiff, secured the trailer to the truck's hitch, and headed off towards the public boat ramp in Everglades City.

The Naples lunch crowd hadn't yet arrived, and there was no activity at the Rod & Gun Club's registration desk, so Jasper was doing what he liked to do best; sitting in a comfortable old chair in the large lanai overlooking the Barron River, watching the lazy boat traffic pass by. The Barron was about a hundred feet across where the Rod & Gun Club bordered it. Since there were plenty of docks and moored boats in the area, this part of the river was designated a *No Wake* zone. Pleasure boats and commercial fishing boats alike puttered to and fro, saving their energy for the channel where they could open up their throttles and fly across the calm waters surrounding the Ten Thousand Islands. The small, overpowered flats boats always reminded Jasper of hunting cheetahs, creeping along until they were within striking distance, and then letting go with an explosion of speed and power. And on this weekend morning Jasper had already counted a half dozen of these cheetah craft as well as a handful of stone crab and blue crab boats. The crab boats were about thirty feet long, held a crew of three or four, and were piled high in the stern with traps and buoys. The Everglades City fishing boats were unique in their design. Most had a characteristic out-house shaped pilot's cabin and bridge which was slanted just a tad towards the bow of the vessel. All were made of wood and in most cases were named after the fisherman's wife or mother. Jasper waved slowly to the captain of the Alice II as it passed by the Club on its way to the Gulf.

Jasper knew all of the local fishing guides and quite a few of the regular recreational fishermen, at least by sight, so he did plenty of waving and nodding during his river watch sessions. Following closely in the wake of the Alice II was a Carolina Skiff powered by a newer model Yamaha 90 horsepower outboard. U.S. Fish and Wildlife officer Dean Applegate was sitting behind the center console at the controls and nodded to Jasper as he pushed by, leaving just enough of a wake to rattle some of the moored boats against their pilings like anxious racehorses in the starting gate.

There was nothing unusual about seeing Applegate heading out on a weekend fishing trip Jasper thought, except that he had never seen him go out alone before. While Jasper was rolling that image through his mind, the sound of an obnoxiously clinking bell grabbed his ear, and he realized there was a customer in need of assistance at the registration desk. Jasper moved quickly for a man in his seventies but the persistent customer continued to pound on the old fashioned silver-plated service bell until Jasper appeared.

"Can I help you?" Jasper said to the yuppie couple standing at the counter.

"Yes. I sure hope so. We drove all the way here from Naples for lunch and your sign says no credit cards," the husband said with surprised concern.

"That's right. No credit cards or personal checks," Jasper replied with a soft smile. "But I don't make the rules. Just work here."

"Well, maybe you could tell us where there's an ATM so we can get some cash," the wife said, jumping into the conversation.

"I can tell you where you can find a bank machine. But I don't think you're gonna like it much. The nearest one's in Naples," Jasper said extending his hands palm side up. He had been through this situation any number of times before.

"Naples! We just *came* from Naples! You're kidding, right?" the husband said. His face was a shade pinker than it had been minutes before. "There's got to be a bank in town."

"Yes, we have a bank. Two actually. But no bank machine," Jasper said, wanting to end the conversation and get back to the peace of the lanai. "The banks are closed anyway. It's Saturday. The Captain's Table Restaurant around the corner takes plastic and so does the Swamp Pizza Parlor over on 29. You passed it on your way in."

"Amazing. Just amazing. You'd think this was 1897. Not 1997," the husband said as he grabbed his wife's hand. "Let's get out of here and return to civilization."

Jasper just smiled, turned, and strolled back to the seclusion of the screened porch world.

Eight

APPLEGATE HAD JUST PASSED THE OUTWARD BOUND facility which lay nestled on a flat spit of land off the starboard side of his skiff when he flattened the lever-like throttle, lurched the boat quickly into a plane, and skimmed above the water's calm surface like a marble rolling along a glass table top. The decades old Outward Bound compound was the last trace of civilization before the human world was dabbed away by the dozens of finger-like islands that separated Everglades City from the turbid open waters of the Gulf of Mexico. A well-marked, infrequently dredged channel named Indian Key Pass provided safe passage through the Ten Thousand Islands to the Gulf, a distance of about six nautical miles.

Applegate moved quickly through the Pass, expertly tracking the channel markers and avoiding more than a few hidden oyster bars. At one point he had to slow down for the *Manatee,* a fifty foot long Everglades Park Service vessel used to take tourists on a forty-five minute excursion into the mangrove forest of the Ten Thousand Islands. A few of the sun screen and bug repellant-smeared sightseers waved at Applegate as he passed, but their friendly gestures were not returned. Applegate had his gaze fixed on Indian Key, now only a mile or so on the horizon. Once he cleared this ten acre rectangular lump of vegetation, he was officially in the Gulf of Mexico and could steer southeast on a course for Pavilion Key, nine nautical miles in the distance.

Applegate knew to approach the island from the north, where the water surrounding the sand strewn island was deep enough to accept his vessel's shallow hull. As soon as he reached Little Pavilion Key, a long tongue of white sand lapping at the wet sea west of Pavilion Key, he veered slightly north and east, and then circled to starboard to begin his slow approach to Pavilion. He noted that the island was deserted as usual and the only boats he could see were miles off in the Gulf, probably fishing for grouper or triple-tail. He fed the outboard one last gulp of fuel with the throttle, aimed the bow towards the shore, and engaged the power tilt to lift the prop and lower unit of the engine safely above the grinding sand and shell that were now hugging the skiff from below. Applegate took one more quick look around, then tossed the anchor onto the beach. He spent a few minutes shuffling around the skiff, grabbing at buckets and shovel, backpack and water bottle, until he finally had all of his supplies piled into the bow of the small boat. He then hopped out onto the warm sand and leaned over the bow to unload it. He was soon marching south along the thick beach of Pavilion Key's eastern shore, two empty five gallon buckets in each hand and a backpack and small shovel strapped to his broad shoulders. On several occasions he stumbled over one of the hundreds of large dead whelks, some nearly a foot long, that covered the sand like old cobblestones. He

54

cursed these molluscan skeletons, but he never took his eyes off an area of high beach about a quarter mile in the distance. When he reached his place of interest, the beach was nearly fifty yards wide and sloped gradually upward from the water line towards the rich vegetation of the central part of the island. White sand gave way to accumulated gray flotsam which covered only a few feet of the sandy mantle. The gnarled driftwood and waterlogged coconuts quickly succumbed to a fur coat of brown and green sea grasses. Small sea grape bushes, prickly pears, and yuccas followed next and soon yielded to a forest of palms, palmettos, scrubby pines, and a few hardwoods.

Applegate neatly placed his buckets in a pile at the edge of the sea grass, about ten feet from the first moon snail nest marker, and began to dig furiously with his spade.

It took him about fifteen minutes to reach the first egg, which he carelessly broke with a whack of the shovel. The next errant swipe of the thick blade cracked eggs two and three. Seeing the moist yolk and albumin coating the tip of his shovel, he abruptly tossed the digging tool aside, and ducked into the hole until only his legs and one supporting arm were visible from the surface. Handful by greedy handful Applegate removed the stubborn sand from the nest hole until the clutch lay before him like gumballs in a jar. Now Applegate's actions became more deliberate and patient. He knew how fragile sea turtle eggs were, and that a jostled embryo could be dislodged from its yolky attachment—certain death for the embryonic chelonian. Applegate removed one egg after the next from the nest hole and carefully divided them among three five gallon buckets. Seventy-two was the final count, not including the three eggs which were destroyed.

He covered each of the displaced clutches with sand and began the labored hike back to the skiff. He carried two of the buckets on the first trip and returned for the third pail and his other supplies. Within an hour he was loaded and poling the skiff off of the beach towards deeper water. With the outboard screaming behind him and the bow of the skiff knocking at the small waves before him, Applegate grinned as he thought how clever he was and how perfectly he had pulled off the nest heist. Now all he had to do was incubate them in his garage for a couple of months and he'd be financially set for years to come.

"Catch anything, mister?" a pink-skinned, corpulent, pre-teen blurted out as Applegate tied the skiff to the pier back at the Barron River Marina.

"Nope, sonny. Not today. At least not anything worth bringing back," Applegate replied with a forced grin.

"Don't bother the man, Danny," the tourist boy's mother said as she tried to be polite and hurry her son along.

"Awe mom. He don't mind," the boy retaliated. "Do ya mister?"

"No. I don't mind," Applegate said as he headed for his truck and trailer. "I don't mind at all."

While Applegate was busy backing up the trailer and getting it into position, the pink-skinned kid was visually scraping the boat with his nosy eyes.

"What 'cha got in them buckets?" Danny asked when Applegate returned to drive the boat onto the trailer.

"Sand," Applegate said without pausing. He half expected the bucket interrogation once he saw the kid wasn't going anywhere. By this time Danny's mother and little sister were focused on some anoles scurrying around the base of a coconut palm a few yards away.

56

"What for? Why do ya have to take a boat to get sand? We were in Miami yesterday and there was tons of it right on the beach," Danny said, visibly annoying Applegate. "We walked all over it, ya know. Didn't need no boat. Could've carried it right to our minivan."

"It's special sand," Applegate said quickly. "Comes from an island not far away. My wife uses it for planting things."

"Planting? Planting what kind of things?" Danny pestered.

"Plants," Applegate said emphatically. Then he revved up the motor and drove the bow of the skiff onto the rubber rollers of the trailer. Dead center.

"Wow! That was cool," Danny said as he watched Applegate's boat loading technique in amazement. "Where d'ya learn to do that?"

"Comes from experience," Applegate said with a smile. "Gotta go now. Nice chatting with you."

Applegate didn't want to get hung up with this kid, or his family for that matter, so he left all of his gear in the boat, including the egg buckets, and crept out of the parking lot until he was out of sight. Then he secured the boat with a safety strap and gingerly placed the buckets into his pickup. After all was stowed, he double checked the trailer hitch and headed north on Route 29 for the Tamiami Trail.

In twenty minutes, Applegate was back home, and the only captive Kemp's ridley sea turtle eggs in the world were piled in doughnut frosting buckets in an East Naples garage.

"God that was close," Neil Hess whispered to Bobby Baker, the large young man in a T-shirt and cut-offs crouched down beside him in the palmettos. "I damn near shot that bugger. And would've if he pulled anything outta that hole other than turtle eggs. Must be his lucky day."

"Yeah," Baker replied slowly.

Bobby Baker and Neil Hess were petty thieves turned treasure hunters. Actually, they were somewhat more than petty thieves. Hess had spent nearly fifteen of his forty-four years in prison for everything from breaking and entering to armed robbery. He even beat a third degree murder rap once. Baker was his latest side kick. Twenty-four years old and not too bright, the red haired young man with the tattooed forearms had become dependent on the criminally seasoned Hess. They had met on the streets of Miami where they were part of a European tourist rent-a-car scam. They were working for a group of thugs who would target recently arrived European vacationers. One offender would stop sharply in traffic, causing the unsuspecting tourist to crash into his bumper. Once the drivers got out of their cars, it was all over. The Europeans carried lots of cash and jewelry and would turn it over to the thief in the trailing car. Hess and Baker were an especially good team, and despite the cut that the ringleader took, they were doing pretty well. Then the whole thing fell apart recently when a young Swiss traveler with balls decided to resist them. He caught Baker in the left eye with a powerful open handed punch that broke the young crook's zygomatic arch. Then he kicked Hess directly in the groin, dropping him to his knees like a choir boy, but not before Hess squeezed off two shots from his Colt Python .357 magnum. The first shot missed the Swiss fellow entirely and shattered the side view mirror of the car. But the second shot tore through the man's sternum and the mushroomed slug entered his heart. He died slumped over the driver's seat with his feet still on the asphalt.

Baker and Hess quickly collected themselves and headed off in one car. They managed to elude the police and made it to Georgia where they jumped from one cheap motel to another for about a month. They vowed to get out of the armed robbery business for good but neither of them had any marketable skills. Hess was something of a history buff, he had done a lot of reading in jail, and after seeing a story in the newspaper about the discovery of Blackbeard's ship in the waters off of Beaufort, North Carolina, he began formulating a crude plan. They'd do their homework in the public library, figure out some pirating hot spots, and buy a high quality metal detector. Hess figured that even without pirate's treasure, they might do okay scouring popular beaches for change and lost jewelry.

Baker actually liked the treasure seeking idea of Hess's and was eager to pursue his partner's new career choice. They began with some of the Florida East coast beaches like Daytona, Melbourne, and Jupiter. After about a week of monotonous beach combing, they were averaging all of nine or ten dollars a day in loose change and a cheap watch or two. Realizing the biggest thing they were getting was a bad sunburn, they decided to be more aggressive with the treasure seeking part of their plan.

An obscure book about Florida Bay pirating contained a reference to Pavilion Key. Hess found the island on a map, saw that it was part of the Everglades National Park, and put a big red circle around it. "Our next stop," he had told Baker with a sinister grin.

Baker and Hess had been systematically working the beaches of Pavilion Key for over a week when Applegate showed up that Saturday morning. They actually had turned up a few seventeenth century copper and silver coins, but no big stashes. They had set up camp in the thick woods at the center of the island where the chance of being detected was small. They were well aware that it was illegal to remove anything at all from a national park, which was one reason they hoped Pavilion Key still held pirate's treasure after centuries of no one searching for it.

"I thought for sure he was diggin' up something valuable. In the high sand and everythin'," Baker whispered to Hess as Applegate placed a few more eggs into one of his buckets. "Wasn't this one of the spots you had picked for us to check out?"

"Yup. Absolutely. If I were a pirate hiding loot, this spot, and some of the other places I marked off, would be perfect," Hess said. "Above the water line and easy digging."

"So why's he bein' so careful with those eggs? And what's he takin' 'em for anyway?" Baker asked.

"Shit if I know. Maybe he's gonna eat 'em. Question is, how the hell did he know where they were? Far as I know there aren't any egg detectors on the market," Hess said.

"Maybe he's a biologist or somethin'. Didn't ya say they was turtle eggs?" Baker said, wrinkling his eyebrows as he strained his gray matter. "Well, they must be *sea* turtle eggs, right? Maybe he's studyin' sea turtles?"

"Of course they're sea turtle eggs. There sure ain't no freshwater turtles out here, and I can't think of no birds that lay that many eggs. Anyway. I can't imagine no biologist digging up a nest and carting the eggs away in a boat. He's gonna eat 'em or something," Hess said. By this time Applegate was walking back to the skiff with the first load of eggs.

"What are we gonna do?" Baker asked in a normal

tone of voice, since Applegate was now about a hundred yards away, downwind.

"Nothing. We ain't gonna do nothing with this guy," Hess said. "Just wait 'til he goes away. That's all. If he was pulling something worth money outta that hole, we'd kill him and bury him in the woods. But this ain't worth our time."

Once Applegate pushed his boat off of the sand, Baker and Hess got as close as they could under cover of the Pavilion Key foliage. Close enough so Hess could clearly read the registration numbers on the bow of Applegate's skiff with the aid of his binoculars.

"Baker. Write these numbers down as I call them out. You never know when this sort of info might come in handy."

NINE

Hey Lydia, some guy named Noble called this morning from down in the Everglades. Says it's important. I think he said he was a game warden. I left his number on the board," said Steve Proctor, a twenty-six year old graduate student with wire-rimmed glasses and the male field biologist's prerequisite uneven beard.

"Game warden, huh? Like with Game and Fish?" Lydia Phillon said. "Or is he a fed?"

"Sorry doc. Like I said. The number's on the board," Proctor replied. "I was busy on the computer crunching some data and wasn't really paying that much attention to the guy."

"All right. At least you're getting some work done," Lydia said with a sigh. "Guess I'll call this Officer Noble and see what he wants."

Lydia Phillon was a young assistant professor of biology at Florida Atlantic University (FAU) in Boca Raton, Florida. Her research specialty was the ecology of sea turtles—specifically their migratory patterns and breeding behavior. She had been on the faculty of FAU for a little more than three years. Her work was internationally respected, and she had a relatively steady stream of grant money, which made her department head and the deans happy. She had also taken on a couple of master's degree students during the past year. Steve Proctor was one of these students.

In addition to her research responsibilities, Phillon had the academic challenge of teaching introductory biology to nonmajors. A monumental task at any institution, Phillon had excelled in this capacity and was certain she had the assignment for life. Or at least until she got tenure and could pawn the course off on another new assistant professor. Her students loved her and she loved most of them back. Her electric enthusiasm for biology motivated even the most apathetic business major taking biology as a distribution requirement.

Phillon was also naturally beautiful with strawberry blonde hair as thick as sea grass, a finely contoured face that had seen just enough sun to leave a speckling of friendly freckles on her tanned cheeks, green eyes that resembled the tropical shallows of a coral reef, and a firm, well-proportioned body. Her voice was deep and mature and didn't seem to fit her physical appearance. But people got used to it and soon learned it was a good match for her decisive and powerful personality.

"Lydia. When you finish with the game warden and your other calls, can we go over some of this hawksbill data? I've got a few questions," Proctor said. Phillon insisted that her graduate students call her by her first name.

"Okay, Steve. How about after lunch?"

"Sounds good. I'll be right here," Steve said. 'Right here' meaning in Lydia's office. Space was a precious resource at FAU and there was only enough prime office space for one of Lydia's graduate students. Since Proctor was the new student in the lab, he had to share a large room with twenty other first-year master's students in the department, which meant sharing computers, phones, etc. Since Lydia had been at a committee meeting all morning, Proctor was taking advantage of her dormant computer to do his hawksbill-nesting statistical analysis work.

"Think you could wrap things up? So I can make these calls in private?" Lydia said, pointing to the erasable bulletin board on the wall above and to the side of her desk. Pictures of sea turtles, pristine beaches, and sunsets filled in some of the other gaps on her office walls.

"Hey. No problem. I think I'll head over to the caf for some chow. Can I bring you back anything?"

"Nope. I'll be fine," Lydia said with a smile. "Had a big breakfast this morning and a couple of doughnuts at the meeting."

When Steve had gone, Lydia scanned the message board and decided to call Noble first. She wondered why a law enforcement officer was calling her in the first place. And from the Everglades at that. She did get her share of nuisance alligator calls since she also taught the biology majors herpetology course. But none of those calls had ever come from someone named Noble.

"Game and Fresh Water Fish," Linda Baldwin said pleasantly as she answered the phone.

"I'd like to speak with Officer Noble please," Lydia said.

"Who should I say is calling?" Linda asked politely.

"Lydia Phillon. I'm returning his call."

"Okay. I'm going to transfer you. Hold on. And if you get disconnected, his direct number is 555-9213."

Lydia jotted the number down on a Post-It note while she waited for Hal to pick up.

"Hal," Linda yelled across the office. "Transferring a call to you."

"Okay. Thanks. I'll pick up," Hal said as as he reached for the phone on his cluttered desk.

"Hal Noble speaking. How can I help you?"

The voice at the other end of the connection said, "Mr. Noble. This is Dr. Lydia Phillon from Florida Atlantic returning your call."

"Oh yes. Dr. Phillon. Thanks for calling back so quickly. I hope I'm not disturbing you."

"Well. No. I don't think you are. I've got a few minutes before I have to prepare for my next class. What's on your mind?"

"I'm familiar with some of your work," Hal said. "Now, I don't keep up with the scientific journals like I should, but I saw your *Science* article on electromagnetic navigation in loggerheads. And I read that nice piece that *Discover* did on your group last fall. Really enjoyed it."

"Thanks. But how can I help *you*, Officer Noble?"

"Yeah. Right. I'll get to the point," Hal said. "You know a lot about sea turtles and I've got a bit of a sea turtle problem down here in the Ten Thousand Islands. At least I think it's a problem."

"Well if it's a problem with commercial fishermen killing turtles, or something illegal like that, you need to call National Marine Fisheries. Not me," Lydia said, her patience thinning just a bit.

"No. It's nothing like that. Really, it's more of a natural history kind of problem. And I need an expert on sea turtle nesting behavior to consult with. Interested?" Hal said.

"You're being awfully vague, Mr. Noble. What exactly *is* it you want me to consult about?"

"I'd rather not talk about it over the phone if that's

okay. How about meeting me down here in Everglades City? I'd like you to see some of this stuff first hand."

"See some stuff first hand," Lydia mimicked quietly. Her curiosity was tapped but she didn't want to show it. "My schedule's pretty tight for the next month or so. I'm tied up with a summer session. Then I'm off to Costa Rica in September to do some field work. Can it wait 'til the fall?" Lydia asked, figuring if it could wait until then she probably wasn't interested.

"No, it can't wait that long. All I can tell you is that we have a unique situation down here that I think you might be interested in. Publishable stuff," Hal said. Figuring the "P" word would grab the young professor's attention.

"Unique, huh?" Lydia said trying not to sound too eager. "Well, I guess I could come down this weekend. I've got some free time on Saturday. Just had some plans fall through."

"Saturday it is. Can you meet me at the ranger station just north of Everglades City?"

"Sure. I know just where it is. Off of the Tamiami, right?" She had spent some time doing a project with alligators in the Everglades as an undergraduate student at the University of Miami and was familiar with the area.

"Exactly," Hal said.

"What time?" Lydia said.

"Ten AM. And bring a wind breaker. We'll be going out in a boat if that's all right with you."

"Fine with me. Should I pack a lunch? I know there's not much down there in the way of fast food."

"No. Lunch is on me. Tuna salad and corn chips okay with you?"

"Sounds good. I eat anything," Lydia chuckled as she unconsciously twirled some of her hair between the fingers

66

of her left hand. "So I guess I'll see you Saturday at ten," she continued.

"Saturday at ten," Hal said.

"Please call me if anything changes though," Lydia said.

"I will. See you Saturday."

Hal had debated whether or not to get a scientist involved in the Pavilion Key situation, but he thought it in the best interest of the developing investigation to have some hard facts to go along with Jasper's lay observations. It wasn't that he doubted Jasper, it was simply that he wanted to confirm Jasper's information.

Lydia was making good time on her drive south and west through the Everglades. The hot Florida sun was beaming into her four-year old Honda Accord through the wide open sunroof and was fighting a losing battle with the cold air blowing from the cranked up air conditioner. As a kid, Lydia's parents never let her or her two sisters have the windows open while the AC was running. But now that she was an adult, with her own car, it was one of her favorite things to do.

Lydia pulled into the Everglades ranger station ten minutes early, closed the sunroof, and spent just a minute or two fixing her hair. Then she locked up, walked toward the front door, and lightly knocked on the screen door.

"C'mon in," Linda Baldwin said in a slightly raised voice without getting up from her desk. "It's open."

Lydia opened the door and stepped into the linoleum floored office. It was an unremarkable place. There were large detailed maps covering much of the wall space. Most were topographic projections but there were a couple of neat satellite images of the Everglades and Ten

Thousand Islands too. A long hallway ran through the middle of the rectangular building feeding about a half dozen offices to either side like an aorta connected to a series of smaller arteries. Linda Baldwin sat at the large 1960s wooden desk which was just to the left of the front door. She was flipping through a fat Rolodex when Lydia closed the door behind her.

"Hi. I'm Lydia Phillon from Florida Atlantic University. Here to see Officer Noble."

"Oh? I don't think he's expecting anyone. It's Saturday you know," Linda said as she visually dissected Lydia from brow to beltline. She noted Lydia's sparkling green eyes, evenly rounded breasts hiding behind a light blue polo shirt, and smooth hips which were obviously firm beneath a pair of snug khakis. Linda wasn't too happy with the results of her quick study.

"Well. We have an appointment," Lydia said triumphantly. "Ten o'clock." She could tell Linda wasn't pleased to see her but couldn't really figure out why.

"An appointment? With Hal? Are you sure . . ."

Just then Hal's head peeked out into the arterial hallway toward the front door. When he saw the two women talking, he hurried out of his office to them. "Hey. You must be Dr. Phillon! You're a little early," Hal said with a big smile. He figured she would be young, but his mental image of her had been more along the lines of a chunky Dian Fossey.

"Lydia Phillon. A pleasure to meet you," Lydia said as she extended her right hand.

Hal firmly took her hand in his. "Yes. It is a pleasure. Thanks so much for coming down. Guess you've already met Linda?"

"Yes. We met," Linda jumped in. "We were just chatting about the fact that is was Saturday and I thought you were taking the day off."

"Oh. I'm sorry. Forgot to tell you about Dr. Phillon's visit. This was the only time she could come down to Everglades City. Busy teaching up in Boca. Right Lyd . . . I mean Dr. Phillon?" Hal said.

"Please. Call me Lydia. All of my grad students do. I just hate the doctor thing. It's so damn formal. And yes. Weekdays are tough for me to get away. Weekends too, usually. But this seemed so, how did you say it Hal? Unique?"

"Yeah. Unique is what I said . . . I think," Hal replied. Then he continued, "Well, it's getting late. We ought to be going if you're going to get back to Boca by dinner time."

"Oh. Don't worry about that. I don't really have a deadline," Lydia said with a little laugh. She liked Hal immediately and was looking forward to spending the day with him. She knew he had packed her a lunch and was already thinking that she might be able to buy him dinner. Assuming he didn't have other plans, of course.

"Where are you going, Hal?" Linda said anxiously. *Who the hell was this strawberry blonde professor and what was she doing spending the day with Hal?*

"We're doing some field work together. Old Jasper over at the Rod and Gun Club said he's located some sea turtle nests down in the islands. Dr. Phillon is a sea turtle nesting expert and has volunteered to help us identify them. That's all. No big deal really," Hal said. He wasn't exactly trying to hide things from Linda, but he felt strongly that at this stage of the investigation, he wanted to keep the details of the situation contained.

"Anything *I* can help with?" Linda asked confidently. Their pizza dinner date earlier in the week hadn't amounted to much, in the form of romance any way, but at least it was a start. She didn't want to lose ground with Hal, especially to another woman, so she persisted.

"No. I don't think so. If anybody calls just tell 'em I'll be back around mid-afternoon," Hal said as he headed back to his office to grab his keys and a knap sack. The cooler with the lunches and bottled water was already loaded in the boat. Hal took one last look around his office to make sure he hadn't left anything.

An awkward silence filled the front office while Hal was away. Lydia continued gazing at the wall maps and Linda tapped nervously at her computer mouse with her index finger.

"Okay. We're outta here," Hal said as he moved quickly towards the door and held it for Lydia.

"Thanks Hal," Lydia said as she started through the open doorway. Then, turning back, she said, "Nice meeting you, Linda."

Linda simply nodded and turned away.

Hal and Lydia's first stop was the Rod & Gun Club in Everglades City. During the short ride from the Ranger station to the Club, Hal briefed Lydia on the Pavilion Key situation. She listened to Hal's story attentively. Even with amused interest. But she thought to herself that there was no way the old timer was right about the Pavilion Key turtles. As everyone knew, Kemp's ridleys only nested on a single beach. And it was hundreds of miles away in Mexico.

Jasper was on the front steps of the elaborate fishing lodge waiting for them. When Lydia saw the weathered old man with the faded coveralls and tattered ball cap, she was even more certain that this would turn out to be just a fun day of boating with a handsome game warden and his old friend. Nothing more.

Hal made the introductions, and they headed off toward the marina in Chokoloskee, five miles south of Everglades City.

After launching the Game and Fish Commission Boston Whaler, Hal idled the craft through the No Wake Zone surrounding the ancient Calusa Indian shell mound which today was Chokoloskee. Originally, the one hundred and fifty acre island had an elevation of over sixty feet above sea level. A mountain by south Florida standards. But white settlers had leveled most of the shell mound to about twenty feet, built on it heavily, and turned it into the modular-home-laden fishing village of Chokoloskee. Year-round population: three-hundred and fifteen.

Once Hal was in the channel, he opened up the Johnson outboard and raced south and east toward Pavilion Key. Lydia was captivated by the natural beauty and isolation of the area. It was a warm summer morning. The wind which pushed continuously at her face cooled her and filled her lungs with the kind of clean wild air she seemed to never get enough of in Boca. She wanted to tell Hal and Jasper how beautiful it was, but yelling was the only way to get their attention in the deafening turbulence, and yelling would have wasted too much of that precious air. So she sat back in the bow swivel chair and relaxed while Hal piloted the boat towards the Gulf. Jasper stood just to Hal's right with his left hand firmly attached to the center console and his eyes fixed on the horizon.

The Gulf waters were calm and they reached Pavilion Key rather quickly. By the time they landed, secured the boat, and walked south to the spot where they had found the footprints and the nest stick days before, it was just before noon.

"Holy shit! These *could* be ridley eggs," Lydia blurted out as she palmed the broken egg shells and rolled them slowly between her fingers which were shaking with excitement.

"Told ya," Jasper said with a smile. "I know my dang turtles, now. But I don't know 'em like you, miss. One white egg looks just like another far's I'm concerned."

"Hold on a minute," Lydia said, somewhat subdued. "I said *could.* be. What I meant was, they really *look* like ridley eggs. Too small to be from a green or leatherback, but they might be loggerhead. It's very hard to distinguish between ridley and loggerhead eggs. Let's try something."

Lydia then handed the broken shells to Jasper and carefully picked through the sand at the bottom of the nest cavity. She scraped away the top couple of inches and came up with a fist-full of moist sand. Pulling a magnifying glass from her fanny pack, she scrutinized the sand for a minute before yiping, "Bingo! It's a ridley nest!"

"How can you be so sure?" Hal said sceptically. "What could examining the sand possibly tell you?"

"Ridley's are daytime nesters, right?"

"If you say so," Hal said.

"All the ones I've seen comin' up on the beach have been durin' the afternoon," Jasper chimed in.

"Okay. When a sea turtle is laying, there's a lot of moisture and mucus around her vent and coating the eggs," Lydia said in her teaching voice. "Now, what is small, moves fast, and would be attracted to moisture on a hot, semitropical island?"

"Bugs?" Jasper said cautiously.

72

"Correct! Insects! Specifically, dozens to hundreds of small black gnats. The type that hover about a healing cut or the prepuce of a dog or horse."

"Yeah. We call 'em 'puppy pecker flies'," Jasper said, nodding.

"What are you two talking about?" Hal said, exasperated.

"Take a look at this," Lydia said giving Hal the magnifying glass and shoving the handful of sand under his nose.

It took a few seconds for Hal to focus on the crumbly sand, but once he did, numeorus bits of tiny black insect body parts were clearly visible among the sand grains.

"You wouldn't see that many diurnal gnats in the bottom of a loggerhead nest. Loggerheads and all the other Atlantic species nest at night," Lydia said triumphantly. "This *is* a ridley nest. Or should I say *was* a ridley nest. It's just amazing. Amazing."

"Okay. Neat detective work. So what happened?" Hal said. "It doesn't look like the work of a hungry raccoon. And the two other shell rings we found last week are still in place. Probably marking other ridley nests."

Lydia's face turned serious. "Poachers. This is a poached nest. Unfortunately, I've seen many of them in my travels. An animal would have left tracks, and lots of empty egg shells. Whatever emptied this nest covered its tracks pretty well and carried the bulk of the eggs away. My guess is these two were probably dropped or left because they were damaged," Lydia said confidently.

"From what Jasper and I have read, Kemp's ridleys only nest at that beach in Mexico. Rancho Nuevo, right?" Hal said.

"That's correct. Not counting a few strays now and

then along the Florida and Carolina coasts. And a couple of the Galveston head start critters that have found their way to Padre Island in the last year or two," Lydia said.

"So this seems pretty unusual. Maybe even important?" Hal said.

"If what Jasper says is accurate. And there are multiple nests here on the island. Then this is probably the most exciting discovery concerning an endangered species since that colony of black-footed ferrets was found a couple of years ago," Lydia said.

"Hey. Don't forget about them ivory-bills in the Big Cypress," Jasper said before he could catch himself.

"I heard some of those rumors. But they were *only* rumors," Lydia said. "Here we have some actual proof. Question is, why would someone come all the way out here to dig up sea turtle eggs for food? I'm guessing the answer is, at least partly, that they know exactly what kind of nest they dug up. And they're not planning on eating those eggs," Lydia said. "Let's get some pictures."

Hal had brought what he liked to call his "PHD" (press here dummy) camera along and began taking pictures of the poached nest.

Lydia opened her camera bag and after shooting a roll of thirty-five millimeter film, she clicked on her compact video camera and filmed the nest hole, the egg shells, and the surrounding area.

Although she caught it on tape, she never would recognize that the twitching palmettos about forty feet inland were the result of Bobby Baker and Neil Hess's successful attempt to dodge the panning glass eye of Lydia's hand-held Sony.

TEN

"DINNER'S READY," SUSAN APPLEGATE SHOUTED FROM the kitchen, her voice carrying through the dining room and around the corner into the modern living room, before dying in the thick wooden door to the garage.

"I said I'll be right in for Christ sakes," Dean Applegate yelled back from the garage where he was busy putting the finishing touches on his sea turtle egg incubator.

"All right," Susan replied in a normal tone of voice which was unheard by her husband. She hated yelling, but knew that it would be much worse had she opened the door to the garage and politely told Dean that dinner was on the table. His mood had deteriorated markedly over the last several days—ever since the doughnut bucket fiasco—and now he was busy building some contraption in the garage made of two by fours, heat lamps, and thick plastic sheets. Susan knew better than to ask him what he was up to. If he wanted her to know, he'd tell her.

As a U.S. Fish and Wildlife officer, Dean had easy access to the volumes of material published annually by the U.S. Department of Commerce, the branch of government that formed an umbrella over a number of organizations including the U.S. Fish and Wildlife Service, the National Oceanic and Atmospheric Administration (NOAA), and the National Marine Fisheries Service (NMFS). NOAA Technical Memorandum NMFS-OPR-3 was entitled: *Review of the Kemp's Ridley Sea Turtle Headstart Program.*

Dean had read this eleven page document at least a dozen times, and combined with some of the other pertinent literature, he had become somewhat of an expert on the subject of hatching Kemp's ridleys. For instance, Applegate knew that incubating the eggs at an abnormally elevated temperature would reduce the incubation time from about fifty to forty-five days and all of the hatchlings would be female (sex determination in many reptilian species is incubation temperature dependent). The sooner the eggs hatched, the quicker Applegate could sell them to Greene in Miami. And by producing all females, Applegate would eliminate the possibility of captive breeding by an accomplished hobbyist, thus keeping demand for ridley's high in case he needed to tap the sea turtle well in the future.

In the wild, there is a temperature gradient in a typical sea turtle nest. Thus, both male and female turtles develop. The incubation chamber Applegate built from supplies he purchased at Home Depot kept the sand and egg-filled doughnut buckets at a uniform eighty-five degrees Fahrenheit. Applegate couldn't be sure when the eggs would hatch, since he didn't know the exact day the eggs were laid. But based on the immaturity of the two eggs that broke on the Pavilion Key beach, he estimated having baby turtles in about six weeks.

While Applegate was tinkering with his incubator, Hal and Lydia were dropping Jasper off at the Rod & Gun

Club. Their return trip from Pavilion Key was uneventful, except for the fact that Lydia couldn't stop talking about the ridley nests, and how important this find was and so on.

She sounds like a dang school girl after her first date, Jasper thought, but he understood her excitement. He even *liked* the young scientist. Sea turtles were her passion, and she had just stumbled upon the biggest sea turtle story of the decade (with the help of good ol' Jasper, of course). He knew that one day the Pavilion ridleys would be discovered. It just seemed more and more likely that *he* wouldn't be around to see it. But he was. And he was dealing with it as best he could. He trusted Hal, and since Hal had enlisted Lydia, he trusted her too.

"Very nice meeting you, Dr. Phillon," Jasper said in the most polite voice he could muster while he tipped his ball cap.

"Call me Lydia. Please," she said quickly with a smile. "An honor and privilege to make your acquaintance. What you've done, telling Hal about the turtles and the trouble with the nest, may help save an endangered species."

"Thanks. But I ain't done nothin'. At least nothin' outta the ordinary," Jasper said. "Hope to see ya again soon."

"I'll call you tomorrow, Jasper," Hal said as Jasper headed slowly up the steps to the lodge.

Jasper turned and smiled. "Less I call you first."

"What a character," Lydia said as they drove away. "How long have you known him?"

"Oh. I guess about seven or eight years. Almost as long as I've been at this job," Hal replied.

"Well," Lydia said with a big smile. "You two make quite a team. Hey, how 'bout I buy you some dinner."

Hal looked instinctively at his watch. Five-thirty. "Are you sure? Don't you have to head back to Boca soon?"

"C'mon. It's early yet. Know any good places?"

"Well. All depends on what you like. Outside of the Rod and Gun Club there isn't much here in Everglades, but I know a neat little spot on the water at Port O' the Islands. Kind of a Cheekee bar restaurant. It's about a fifteen minute drive east towards Naples, but they have the best stone crab claws and cole slaw in the state. And a pretty good beer selection too. . . . that is if you drink beer, I mean," Hal said, pulling up his words quickly.

"Are you kidding? Nothing like washing down spicy crustacean parts with a cold one. The Cheekee bar it is!" Lydia said with a yelp.

As they drove towards the ranger station Hal prayed that Linda was no longer in the office. Things had been a little awkward between them lately. She was obviously interested in him and he was always too busy to spend time with her. Now he was getting ready to have dinner with a woman he had met just eight hours earlier.

Linda's car was gone.

"I'm just gonna unhitch the boat and get things cleaned up a little," Hal said as they got out of the Blazer. "Then we can go."

"Sounds good. Mind if I use the bathroom in the office?" Lydia asked.

"No problem. Here's the key to the front door," Hal said, handing Lydia his key chain with the proper key exposed. Her fingers brushed his palm and seemed to linger for just a second, like a butterfly tasting a flower, before they pulled away holding the keys.

Hal spent a few minutes dislocating the trailer from the Blazer and cleaning the outboard and hull with fresh water. Lydia reappeared in the parking lot just as Hal was finishing.

"Why don't I drive? After all, I'm taking *you* out to dinner," Lydia said.

"Okay. But you'll need me to navigate."

"Deal. Let's go, navigator."

Although Hal ate at the Port O' the Islands outdoor restaurant on occasion, he didn't know the waitress who seated them. And there was no waiting line since it was off season. A wonderful breeze was blowing off of the Faka-hatchee canal and across the small dining tables located under the rustling dried palm fronds that formed the roof of the Cheekee.

The Port O' the Islands was a combination housing development, resort hotel, and miniature airport. Twenty miles east of Naples, it had never really caught on as a popular vacation spot, but there was enough regular business from the Miami traffic to keep the place going, and almost all of the new construction houses and condominiums had sold. Port O' the Islands sort of came alive in the winter, after Thanksgiving, but the summer months were pretty quiet.

"Follow my finger," Hal said, his outstretched right arm pointing towards the canal about forty feet away.

"Okay. What am I looking for?" Lydia asked hesitantly.

"Just keep your eye on the spot where I'm pointing. You'll see," Hal said confidently.

"Hey! A manatee! No. Two manatees!" Lydia said excitedly. "Wow. I haven't seen one in years."

"Yeah. They put on quite a show here. Especially in the winter when the water in the canal is about ten degrees warmer than the Gulf.

Just then the waitress returned with silverware, place settings, and two glasses of water.

"What can I get you to drink?" The twenty-something

woman said. She was polite enough. Perky even. Wearing tan dockers and the Hawaiian shirt pattern which all of the waitpersons and bar tenders seemed to have on.

"What's on tap?" Lydia jumped in.

"Bud. Bud light. And a local micro brew called Swamp Ale," the waitress replied.

Lydia looked across the small table at Hal. "How's the Swamp Ale?"

"Well. It's a little strong. Unusual . . . in a way. But if you haven't had it before it's probably worth try. . . ."

Lydia had heard all she needed to know, "We'll have a pitcher of the Swamp Ale."

"And a dozen stone crab claws plus a big bowl of cole slaw," Hal added. "Sound okay?"

"Sounds better than okay," Lydia said, staring at Hal for just a second longer than necessary.

Half the pitcher was gone before the food even arrived, and Lydia was drinking the bulk of it. She lived by the work hard play hard credo. And while she didn't drink frequently, she had a tendency to cut loose a little after a day in the field. Old graduate school patterns were tough to erase.

When the waitress brought the pile of chilled crab claws, fresh bread, and cole slaw to the table, Lydia was giggling and her eyes sparkled like the moonlight skipping across the small Fakahatchee waves close by.

Hal was pretty much mesmerized by her. He hadn't felt this way in a while. Not since Alison. And he was so absorbed by her casual but bouncy personality that he had forgotten about Pavilion Key and the ridleys for the moment. Had he had a conversation like this one recently? Ever? They took turns trading anecdotes and each listened to the other intently. No competition. No one-upmanship. Just meaningful and fun story sharing. They avoided talk

80

of past relationships and similar messy topics, but it soon became clear that there was no one at home waiting up for either of them.

"Did you know that stone crabs don't die so we can eat them?" Hal said as he picked some flaky crab flesh from its chitinous cave.

"What do you mean they don't die? They look dead to me," Lydia said with a laugh as she dipped a completely intact crab claw muscle into a small bowl of special mustard sauce. "You don't need to try and make me feel better about it. This is heaven and I'm not going to worry about the little crabs right now."

"No. Really. I'm not kidding," Hal persisted. "Look. Just claws, right?

"Yeah," Lydia said.

"Well, in Florida, the fishermen can legally only take a single claw from crabs that meet the minimum size standard. So the crabs are tossed back with one good claw. They say it's enough for them to survive."

"Serious?" Lydia asked, taking a big gulp of Swamp Ale. "Don't they bleed to death?"

"Nope. They have these little built-in fracture planes to escape predators in the wild," Hal said. "So when enough pressure is placed on the claw, it snaps off and the blood vessels automatically seal. I mean, they lose a little blood, but not enough to kill them."

"Pretty amazing. But what do you think about it?" Lydia asked. "Do they survive?"

"Oh. I'm sure a lot of them don't. Takes a couple of years to grow a functional limb back," Hal said. "But a few probably make it. The biggest problem is poachers. Greedy fisherman taking *both* claws. They get caught once in a while, but it's tough to prove."

As the crab claw conversation continued, the waitress

arrived at the table and began removing the empty shells and crumpled paper napkins. "Can I get you another pitcher?" she asked.

"Sure," Lydia said quickly. "Another pitcher of that Swamp Ale."

"Um. Lydia. Do you think that's such a good idea?" Hal said quietly. "I mean. You've got a long drive ahead of you and it's nearly eight-thirty."

"Of course. You're right. I probably should be ordering coffee," Lydia said with a smile. She was kind of hoping Hal would offer her a place to stay so she wouldn't have to make the late night drive back to the east coast. The truth was she was having so much fun she didn't want the evening to end.

"Well, now. Lydia. I'm not trying to tell you what to do. I just want you to be safe and everything," Hal said, cautiously dipping his big toe into the waters of their developing relationship.

The amused waitress was still standing by the couple, pen and paper in hand. She heard their entire conversation, and finally chimed in, "why don't you just spend the night at his place and have another beer?"

Everyone was silent for a moment. Even the waitress. What a bold thing to say she thought as she monitored Lydia and Hal for their reactions.

Lydia blushed noticeably and Hal looked up at the young waitress in disbelief. "Well. . . . I do have a guest room. You could stay there. . . . ," Hal said breaking the silence. "Maybe it's not such a bad idea."

"Oh, Hal. I wouldn't want to be any troub. . . ."

"No. Really. It wouldn't be any trouble at all. I mean the place is a little messy. But this way you could get a fresh start in the morning. Be in Boca in time for church."

"I don't go to church much," Lydia chuckled. "But if you're sure it's no trouble, I'll take you up on the offer."

"So another pitcher?" the waitress said smiling.

"How 'bout a frosty mug for Lydia here," Hal said. "I'll just have some iced tea and be the designated driver. That is if you don't mind me driving your car?"

"Perfect!" Lydia said. Then, addressing the waitress, "can we take our drinks down by the water? It looks so nice over there where the mangroves meet the canal."

"Sure. Folks do it all the time," the waitress said. "I'll bring your drinks in plastic cups." Then she turned and headed for the kitchen. She couldn't wait to tell her co-workers how she had fixed up the couple eating the crab claws.

"You must love it here—getting to work outside and in such beautiful country," Lydia said as they walked single-file down the serpentine path leading to the canal's edge.

"I probably don't enjoy it enough," Hal said. "I love the outdoor work. And the scenery. But I'm usually so focused on one thing or another; the current project; a particular poacher; that I rarely close up shop and take it all in anymore. But tonight—this moment—talking with you. . . ." Hal cut himself off like a batter taking a check swing at a ball that looked hittable but then curved away at the last second. "I really need to do this more often," he said, opting for the safe base on balls.

"Well. I'm glad that you're having fun," Lydia said as they broke through the mangroves to an open area where several large but smooth pieces of coralline rock sat like sleeping tortoises on the canal's mucky bank. "Why don't we sit down for a bit?"

Hal and Lydia were soon perched atop their limestone seats, staring out across the calm, murky water fill-ing the man-made canal and evenly set mini-harbors where home owners docked their water craft. The moon was bright and full. Thin gray clouds passed across its face like ghosts trying to escape a spotlight. A chuck-will's-widow called from somewhere deep in the mangroves.

"So. Who the hell's digging up the ridley nests?" Lydia said at last, the Swamp Ale doing a good job of eroding her inhibitions. It was somehow understood that both of them were thinking about Pavilion Key.

"It's a tough one. Most of the time it's pretty easy to figure out a poacher's motives. Wildlife collectors are in it for the quick buck. Hunters are the same, but sometimes they just need meat for the freezer. Then there's just the plain old bored, mean ones. Those people, the malicious ones, they're usually not too smart. And pretty lazy. Odds are heavy against one of them schlepping the thirty miles out to Pavilion Key and back to eradicate a sea turtle nest."

Lydia was now giggling out loud. "Schlepping. I love it. Haven't heard that word in years," she said smiling. As she listened to Hal talk, she found herself caught up in his passion. Like an insect trapped in a spider's web. She hoped the seemingly shy game warden would see that she was taken by him—maybe even make the first move. But it seemed unlikely. The insect would have to attack the spider, she thought.

They continued to mull over the Pavilion Key conundrum for another thirty minutes or so. By this time Lydia's plastic cup was empty. "Maybe we should head back to your place? It's nearly ten."

"Sure. Yeah. I get pretty carried away sometimes," Hal said standing up.

Lydia also got up and they walked slowly towards the

Cheekee Hut along the mangrove path. When they were inside of the mangrove thicket, and still out of sight of the restaurant, Lydia reached for Hal's right hand with her left and clutched it. Lydia's hand felt warm and strong—the gesture pleased Hal. They turned and faced each other and Lydia soon found herself taking Hal's other hand and stepping up on her toes to kiss him.

The first kiss was short and a little dry. Their lips met unevenly like a jigsaw puzzle piece being positioned in the wrong space. They stepped back and looked at each other for a moment—long enough for a breath—and then embraced in a much longer and wetter kiss that filled them both with the tinglings of lust.

The warm Swamp Ale and coconut lip balm flavor combination that rolled over Hal's tongue and along his lips and cheeks was making his heart race. Hal was becoming aroused by a woman for the first time in months. He was sure the pounding pump in his chest was rocking Lydia's breasts, which were firmly pressed against his rib cage. Or was it *her* heart beat that he was feeling?

When their flushed faces finally parted, they stared at each other for a few moments. They were both breathing heavily and their eyes were sparkling with excitement and the anticipation of the next kiss.

Hal broke the short silence which had been punctuated by the sound of air moving quickly in and out of their nostrils, "Ummm. . . . okay. . . . should we go back to the car?"

"Definitely," Lydia said. "But I'll only go if you kiss me again."

ELEVEN

"Bobby boy. There is some *shit* going down on this island," Neil Hess said to Baker after Hal, Jasper, and Lydia were safely out of range. "Some *real* funny shit."

"What d'ya mean boss?" Baker said matter of factly. "Just a game warden and some friends is all if ya ask me."

"First of all, I wasn't asking you. I was telling you! There's something to these turtle nests. I can feel it. But I just can't pin it down. Let's go over this once. Okay?"

"Okay."

"So. We got a guy. Works for Fish and Wildlife. Comes way out here to Pavilion Key and digs up a nest full of eggs. Then, handling 'em like they're new born children, he puts 'em in buckets and carts 'em outta here. Then. Next day. This state game warden, a chick, and an old cracker show up on Pavilion looking at the looted nest and wandering around trying to figure out what the hell happened."

"Maybe they know each other?" Baker said. "Maybe they just got their days mixed up."

"Think so?" Hess snarled sarcastically. "Come on you idiot. That first guy was working alone. I could tell. Now, it's possible they know each other. But I can tell you right off they're not playing for the same team."

"Well, I wrote all the numbers down like ya told me boss," Baker said, trying to pull a positive response from Hess's mouth. "Got em right here in my pocket."

"Good. Hang on to 'em and don't lose 'em," Hess said. "I can't figure out why, but these turtle eggs might have some value. And if they're valuable to other folks. . . . they might be valuable to us."

"Ya know, boss, I saw a TV show a while back 'bout sea turtles. The guy on the TV said they're pretty endangered. Ya know. Not many are left. Most of 'em were wiped out for food years ago. And now lots of 'em get stuck in fishin' nets. Or maybe it was shrimp nets. Anyway, they drown and these folks on the show were tryin' to protect 'em by makin' the fishermen use these special kinds of nets so the turtles could swim out of the net without drownin'. Then—"

"What the hell are you rambling on about?" Hess yelled, cutting Baker off. "I know all about the poor sea turtles, and the shrimping industry. And who the hell cares about 'em except a bunch of blue haired old ladies and a few tree huggers. Greenpeacer's and the like. These people don't *want* the turtles. They just want to save 'em so the stinky reptiles can go on pissing in the sea and getting caught up in fishing tackle."

"Maybe some people *do* want the turtles?" Baker said quietly, knowing that Hess would shoot him down again. "Baby sea turtles are pretty cute. I saw 'em on TV running across the sand for the water and all these people were helping 'em get there. Kind of pickin' 'em up like little wind up toys and droppin' 'em into the waves. Bet they'd make pretty good pets. Least 'til they got real big."

"Pets! Sea turtle pets! Yeah, that's probably it, Bobby. You could put 'em in a mayonnaise jar and feed 'em 'til they burst out, spraying glass all over the damn place."

"Boss. Ya wouldn't have to put 'em in a may'naise jar. You could put 'em in a big bucket. Or a trash can. Maybe the bath tub," Baker said as his mind explored the possibilities. "Maybe Sea World would want 'em?"

"I'm sure Sea World has *plenty* of turtles," Hess said. "They're always on the news rescuing this and that and then dumping it into one of their trillion gallon tanks for the public to ogle over. Nope. The pet idea is out. But it still doesn't mean they're not valuable. Who knows? Those orientals might put the little buggers into their green tea to help 'em get hard-ons. They do that kinda shit ya know. Saw it on Twenty-Twenty."

"So. What are we gonna do? Keep lookin' for pirate's treasure?" Baker said. "Or should *we* dig up some of 'em eggs for us?"

"We're not digging up any goddamn eggs, Baker. At least not yet. We're nice and settled here on Pavilion, so it won't hurt to keep an eye on this part of the beach for a while. You never know who might turn up next sniffing around these turtle nests. I say we shift our treasure hunting to this part of the island for a week or two."

"Sounds good to me. I'm beginnin' to think there isn't no treasure at the south end of the island anyway."

Baker and Hess moved their camp from the southern part of the island to a small clearing in the thick subtropical forest about two hundred yards from the spot where Applegate had dug up the ridley nest. They kept a small Zodiac in camp which they used every week or two to motor to Chokoloskee for supplies. One of the pair always remained behind to keep an eye on the camp. Hess was convinced there was buried treasure somewhere on the island, but he was also hoping that something would pan out with the sea turtle nest situation. As July boiled over into August, their diligent metal detecting hadn't turned up anything of value, and the Fish and Wildlife guy hadn't returned to dig up any more nests.

On three separate occasions during the month of July, about once a week as far as they could tell, the game warden and the old cracker visited Pavilion Key. The visits were short, usually less than thirty minutes, and consisted of nothing more than a walk by the spot where the sea turtle nest had been destroyed in June. On one occasion, when Hess was off in Chokoloskee buying supplies, the game warden and the young woman who they had seen that first time visited Pavilion, but nothing remarkable happened. They just walked up the beach to the same spot, looked around a bit, then headed back to their boat. Hess was concerned that they might have seen Baker, but Baker assured him that he was well concealed in the thick island brush and that he had only observed them from a distance through his binoculars. He was telling the truth.

But Hess was getting worried. His confidence was eroding like the thin beach on Little Pavilion Key. And Baker grew more impatient with each setting sun. Hess was sure his reluctant partner was ready to toss in the shovel and head back to Miami any day. What they needed was some luck, he thought. A break.

The luck he wished for was on its way.

TWELVE

ALTHOUGH LYDIA DID SPEND THAT FIRST NIGHT AT HAL'S on the couch, their relationship progressed to the daily phone call and weekend sleepover stage very quickly. It was the fastest Hal had ever become involved with a woman. And he loved it. Lydia was completely uninhibited and she brought a submerged part of Hal's persona to the surface which rarely floated free.

He still hadn't told Linda or the other folks at the Ranger station about his relationship with Lydia. But there were rumors.

"Hey. You're reading *The Windward Road*!" Lydia exclaimed excitedly with just a touch of surprise as she eyed the bright orange hardcover with the black print that was lying atop a pile of magazines on Hal's kitchen counter. There was a scrap-paper bookmark wedged between pages of the first chapter. "Where did you get hold of it?"

"Collier County Public Library," Hal said. "Figured since I'd be hanging around with a sea turtle expert, I better learn a little more about 'em. I assume you've read it?"

"*Read* it? I've read *all* of Archie Carr's stuff," Lydia said, a radiant smile crossing her face. "And *The Windward*

Road's about my favorite. But it looks like you haven't gotten very far on it."

"Oh, the bookmark," Hal said as he glanced over at the 1956 tome. "I actually finished it last night, but wanted to reread that first chapter, *The Riddle of the Ridley.*"

"It's been a while since I read the book," Lydia said. "That's the chapter where he talks about how, at the time, no one knew where the ridley's came from. Right?"

"Yup. It's pretty amazing when you think about it," Hal said as he walked over to the counter and picked up the book. He quickly flipped from page to page until he located the spot he was looking for. "For instance, listen to this neat passage when Carr and a Caribbean turtle fisherman named Jonah Thompson have just boated a ridley in 1937. The first time Archie Carr ever saw a live ridley. Do you mind if I read it to you?"

"No. Go ahead. I'd love it," Lydia said.

"Okay," Hal said. And he began to read in his best narrator's voice.

> *"Stay clear of him," Jonah said. "He's mad. Ridleys is always mad."*
>
> *I poked a rope end at the turtle's face. It seized the knot and crunched and then flew into a long frenzy of flopping and pounding about the deck.*
>
> *"You can't keep a ridley on its back. Only a few hours. They're crazy. They break their hearts."*
>
> *That was how I got to know the Atlantic Ridley. That was how the great ridley mystery began for me.*

"Pretty cool stuff. Doesn't Carr talk a bit about how the turtle got its name?" Lydia said, leaning over Hal's shoulder with her chest pressed lightly against his back.

"Yeah. It's right here," Hal said. And he continued reading.

It was eighteen years ago when Jonah Thompson pulled in that first ridley out at Sandy Key in Florida Bay. I was there because of a letter from my friend Stew Springer, who is a gifted naturalist, versed in all sorts of seacraft. He was running a shark fishery at Islamorada on the upper Florida Keys at the time. He wrote to me to complain about a kind of turtle his fisherman brought in for shark bait. It was an evil-natured turtle, he said, flat and gray, with a big head and short, broad shell. Unlike the docile greens, which lie for weeks back-down on a ship's deck, or the formidable but philosophical loggerheads, this species made an unrestful, even dangerous, boatfellow. It snapped and fought, Stew said, from the moment it fell over the gunwale, biting the air and slapping its feet till it burned itself out from rage and frustration. The people on the keys called it ridley, and Stew said he could not even find the name—much less any information on it—in any of the books.

Neither could I. From the description I decided that Stew must be talking about a species that was first described some sixty years ago as Lepidochelys kempi, *the specific name being taken from that of Richard Kemp of Key West, who sent the type specimen to Samuel Garman at the Museum of Comparative Zoology at Harvard. Practically nothing was known about the natural history of Kemp's turtle. Most people were unable to distinguish it from the loggerhead, and many even doubted that there really was such a thing. A scattering of herpetologists had published records of its occurrence or comments on its osteology, but the great majority of reptile students had never even seen one and the general attitude was that Kemp's turtle was a somehow inferior, if not altogether spurious form, not worthy of scholarly sweat.*

"Archie had his wife along on that 1937 outing with Jonah Thompson. Check this part out," Hal said. Lydia followed along in the text as Hal read aloud.

And so, when he contemplated the irate ridley he had just pulled up on deck and said: "Some say these ridleys is crossbreeds," I took notice and urged him on.

"Is that Jonah Thompson saying they were crossbreeds?" Lydia asked trying to keep track of the dialogue.

"Yeah. Jonah's talking and Carr is urging him to continue." Hal said.

"We don't know where they lay," he said. "All the rest come up on the beaches one time or other, but you never see the ridleys there. We all say they are made when a loggerhead pairs with a green." He mumbled something else in an embarrassed sort of way. I thought I heard him right, but I didn't think my wife did.

"We think they're so damn mean owing to them not getting to coot none," was what I believe he said.

"What did he say?" asked Margie.

"Shut up," I said.

"Did he say they are mean because they don't make love?"

"That was the gist of it."

"Isn't that anthropomorphic?" Margie asked, in an unpleasant way.

"Could be," I said. I could see nothing wrong with the man's reasoning, provided he was right about the ridley's not breeding; but this assumption I did not like, and still don't.

It bothered me that the ridley should be such a distinctive and original-looking creature, with his traits his own and nothing about him that seemed intermediate between the other species. A mule is clearly a mixture of the ass that sired him and the mare that bore him, but a ridley is his own kind of animal. I nodded over Jonah Thompson's theory, but I resolved then to get the straight of it somehow.

As I said, that was a long time ago, and I have made very little progress. Indeed, the ridley mystery has grown rather than shrunk, and I am farther from a solution than I seemed then. The answer is so elusive that I have come to regard the ridley as the most mysterious air-breathing animal in North America.

"When Carr wrote this book, they weren't even sure if the ridley was an *actual* species," Hal said. "Listen to this."

When the turtlers and fisherman are pressed to account for the facts of the case, they tell three different stories. Most of them agree with Jonah Thompson that the creature does no breeding on its own but is produced when two other species hybridize. The comment of an old pod at St. Lucie Inlet was the sort of thing you hear:

"This yer ridley don't raise. He's a bastard, a cross-breed you get when a loggerhead mounts a green—and a loggerhead will mount anything down to a stick of wood when he's in season. This yer ridley don't have no young'uns. He's at the end of the line, like a mule."

94

*A minority among the people I talk to say that rid-
leys breed all right—bound to; everything does; but they
do it somewhere 'way off, outside our field of responsibil-
ity. On some remote shore of the Caribbean, maybe,
where they have yet to be observed by sapient man. Sapient gringo, anyway.*

"The rest of the chapter talks more about the puzzle of
the ridley and Carr's attempts over a fifteen year period to
figure out the natural history of the turtle," Hal said
thumbing ahead a few pages. "But you've got to hear these
last two paragraphs."

*What remains to be done, then, is slow, piecemeal
searching. And before I look anywhere else I am going
back to Florida Bay—to the shallow, island-set sea between the cape and the upper keys. There are dozens of
little islands there like Sandy Key, and they have been
little visited by naturalists with eyes open for ridley sign.
The shores there are mostly mangrove thickets, where no
turtle could nest; but in some the mangrove fringe is
broken by sand; and while the strips of beach are short
and narrow, they may be all the ridley needs. The bay is
handy to both the Florida Current, which must be the
agent that feeds the waifs into the Gulf Stream, and to
the coastal waters of the peninsula of Florida, where ridleys are more abundant than anywhere else. It is at least
possible that the natural secretiveness of sea-turtle hatchlings keeps baby ridleys out of sight, and that some local,
seasonal migration of the egg-heavy females hides them
from view. All this seems unlikely, but it is the most possible solution at hand.
So I guess I should have stayed on there in the bay to*

95

look for the answer, where Jonah Thompson threw the iron so long ago. Perhaps all the Atlantic ridleys everywhere come from down there where the first one was, in the hot, white water with the sea cows and bonefish and the last crocodiles. Maybe the long questing will come full circle there on some first full moon of summer, and the riddle of the ridley will end where it began.

"God. So Carr wasn't all that far off with his Florida Bay theory," Lydia said, her voice jumping about. "I mean. Pavilion Key isn't *that* far north of Cape Sable."

"About forty miles," Hal said. "Wonder if Carr ever got up this way looking for ridleys?"

"I know the scoop on that, Hal. Not long after *The Windward Road* was published, word of the Rancho Nuevo find reached Carr and the other prominent US herpetologists. There was no need to look any further. As far as Carr and the others were concerned, the riddle of the ridley had been solved. The world's only Kemp's ridley nesting beach had been identified."

"That's what they thought, anyway," Hal said.

"Yeah. That's what we *all* thought. Until *this* summer," Lydia said. "I sure wish Archie Carr were still alive. He'd really get a kick out of the Pavilion ridleys."

"I bet he would. And look at this," Hal said excitedly as he flipped to one of the black and white maps that appeared in the front of the book. "Pavilion Key and Rancho Nuevo. They're located on practically the same latitude."

While Lydia and Hal were ogling over Carr's *The Windward Road* and each other, Dean Applegate was becoming increasingly anxious with each passing July day. Based on his calculations, the turtles should have started hatching some time during the third week of the month. Especially with the help of the elevated temperatures in his garage-protected incubator. But not a single grain of sand in the buckets had moved. And Winslow Greene in Miami had already called several times inquiring about the hatchlings. He already had Japanese and European buyers for nearly two dozen of them. Applegate was starting to get pressure from the Marco Island real estate agent who was planning on selling him that beautiful lot near the Snook Inn with the fabulous view of the Marco channel and the nearby Isles of Capri. Plus the contractor he had talked to about building his dream house on the Marco lot kept calling at work to see when ground could be broken. And he hadn't even *bought* the damn lot yet—couldn't until he had the ridley money in hand.

The nesting beach on Pavilion Key was as quiet as Applegate was agitated during the latter part of July. Hal and Jasper had made several trips to Pavilion Key during the month and noted no further disturbances around the nesting area. Lydia was able to manage only one trip to Pavilion during the month, a Saturday picnic excursion with Hal.

But there *were* some unusual developments on Pavilion Key during those hot July days. And they had nothing to do with sea turtles. Neil Hess and Bobby Baker had finally found something in the sand.

THIRTEEN

AH, CRAP," BOBBY BAKER SAID AS THE SMALL, BLUE-flame dimples of the burner on the Coleman stove flickered and died, like little prairie dogs being sucked back into their holes. "That's it for the propane. Now what'll we do?"

"Quit your whining. You're a real pussy, you know it?" Neil Hess shouted as he rolled out of the two-man tent and zipped up the mosquito screen behind him. "Guess we'll just have to make a fire. Or eat our eggs raw. You pick."

"Hey. I'm not a pussy. I just don't like campin'," Baker said. "It's dirty. The bugs are bitin' the shit out of me. And the food sucks."

"See what I mean? You're nothing but a big pussy whiner. Hell. You could be sitting in a Miami jail cell right now. What do you think of that?"

"I think it might be better than this. Least the food be okay," Baker replied. "And no damn 'skitoes bitin' my ass all the time."

"Well you ain't in Miami. And you ain't in jail. You're

stuck on this lump of hot sand with me. And we're staying here 'til we find some damn treasure or something," Hess said. "Our luck's gotta change."

It was now the first Saturday in August on Pavilion Key. Baker and Hess finished breakfast, and as they had planned the night before, headed to some high ground beach near the north end of the island. Not far from the turtle nesting spot.

"Here. You take this damn thing," Hess said, handing Baker the bulky metal detector. "I'll carry the shovel for a change."

"Okay," Baker said reluctantly as he fastened the cushioned headphones about his ears like a scared little-leaguer putting on a batting helmet. "I'll give it a shot."

Baker and Hess followed the gliding head of the metal detector as it scanned the rippled sand like a sea skate moving to and fro searching the bottom for molluscan morsels. Baker occasionally bounced the circular plastic disc off of driftwood hunks and tufts of beach grass, triggering contact beeps which were nothing more than false alarms. The detector they were using was designed for underwater use, which meant it worked great in the surf and very moist areas, but it had the annoying tendency to beep when it struck anything from the side.

But then a faint beep tickled Baker's eardrums when the scanner was over clean sand. It wasn't a false alarm. And the discriminator knob was set fairly high. Which meant the chance that the beep represented a bottle top, flip tab, or other piece of trash was unlikely. No. This was a legitimate signal.

Baker carefully scanned the area again. More slowly this time. In an effort to pinpoint the source of the signal.

"What's up?" Hess said, noticing that Baker had stopped and was passing the detector over and over the same small area.

"I think I've got something," Baker said loudly, the headphones betraying the volume of his voice.

"You don't gotta yell, goddamnit," Hess snarled. "I'm standin' right here."

"Oh. Sorry. It's these darn earphones," Baker said sincerely. "I feel like I'm in a tunnel when I wear 'em."

"Give me the damn thing," Hess said impatiently, grabbing at the metal detector. "I'll mark the spot and *you* can dig."

Baker turned the metal detector over to Hess and took the small shovel.

"Here's the spot," Hess said, waving the disc over a place in the sand he had marked with the toe of his right foot. "Start digging."

Baker dug for a few minutes, like a dog in slow motion, until he had produced an even pile of sand about a foot high and two feet wide.

"Okay. Step back and let me check it," Hess snapped. Then he slowly passed the detector's head over the small pile of sand. Nothing. Next he passed the detector over the fresh hole, allowing the plastic disc to dip into the depression as it swept by. "Yow!" he yelled. "Now *that's* a signal. Whatever it is, it's still in the ground. Keep digging!"

Baker saw how excited Hess had become and this time he attacked the hole like a prisoner digging for freedom. Within five minutes he had doubled the diameter of the hole and it was now eight inches deeper. The sand actually felt cold as he smoothed out the cavity with his bare hands. And there seemed to be less sand and more dirt at this depth.

Again, Hess checked the newly excavated sand with the detector. No signal. But when he let the plastic disc drop into the hole, the signal in his ear was the loudest yet. Even Baker, standing a few feet away, heard it through the headphones.

"We're getting close. So dig a little more slowly now," Hess said.

Beads of sweat had now appeared on Baker's brow and forehead. And a few of them had coalesced into a small salty rivulet that trickled down his nose and into his eyes. He wiped the irritating discharge from his face with a swipe of his backhand which was covered with sand and dirt, leaving a gritty brown smudge from his left cheek to his hairline. He used the shovel to loosen up the dirt at the bottom of the hole and his hands to cup the sandy soil out onto the beach.

Then the shovel struck something hard. Not a rock. Not metal either. It felt like wood to Baker. So he put down the shovel and leaned into the hole for a look. Mixed in with the light brown dirt and moist sand was what looked like a small white stick. Then he saw another. And another.

"Well? What the hell is it?" Hess asked anxiously. "What are you fiddling with in there?"

Baker pulled his head and torso out of the hole and turned to look at Hess. His ashen face was in sharp contrast to the sash of dirt and sweat that crossed it. "I think we found someone's hand, boss. At least the finger bones. And there's a big ring attached to one of 'em."

The blank expression on Hess's face didn't change for several seconds. In fact, the two men were fixed in a sort of awkward stare for a moment.

"Finger bones and a ring?" Hess said finally. "Did I hear you right? goddamn finger bones?"

"Have a look for yourself," Baker said, shuffling away from the hole and pointing towards its bottom with his right hand.

Hess knelt down and ducked into the hole, swung his head slowly back and forth like a child bobbing for apples at a carnival game, then reached into the shallow pit and grabbed the section of bone that the ring delicately clung to.

"Will you look at this shit," Hess said slowly. "Will you look at this."

Hess was holding several bones of a human being's left hand (more specifically, the metacarpal bone and first and second phalanges of the ring finger). The weathered, partially decayed bones were still loosely connected by some brown, gristle-like cartilage. The distal, or third phalanx, was gone. At least Hess hadn't picked it up. And a large gold ring with an unusual oblong-cut red stone hung loosely over the first phalanx.

Baker and Hess had discovered the grave of Kaaren van Bokkelen, the young Dutch virgin murdered so long ago by the pirate, Charles Gibbs. When the crew of the U.S. naval vessel *The Porpoise* discovered the young girl's fresh, shallow grave back in 1818, Lieutenant Ramage ordered a new, deeper grave dug for her body. And he insisted that she be buried just as Gibbs had left her. . . . outfitted in a flowing white dress and generously adorned with a variety of beautiful, pirated jewelry. His orders were followed, and she rested undisturbed until now.

"This ring's gotta be worth a shit load of money," Hess said as he tussled lightly with the skeletal finger, pulling the bones apart and dropping them on the sand once he had the ring in his hand. "Get that shovel moving and let's see what else we can find. There's gotta be a body attached to this hand."

"Do ya think that's such a good idea, boss?" Baker said sheepishly. "I mean, what if this is a grave? Ya know. Like maybe someone buried this body here?"

"Like maybe someone buried this body here?" Hess mocked in a rolling, high-pitched voice. "Who the hell cares how the body got here! Start digging and I'll work the detector. With a little luck we'll find some more jewelry on these bones. A couple rings like this will carry us halfway through the winter."

FOURTEEN

I T WAS THE SOUND OF THE CAMERA'S MOTOR DRIVE THAT caught Neil Hess's attention as he and Baker unearthed the last of the Dutch virgin's bones.

"Did you hear that?" Hess said as he stopped digging and looked around.

"I didn't hear anything, boss. Maybe it's the ghost of this girl stirrin' about." By this time Hess and Baker were sure that the skeleton was female. In addition to the ring, they had also found a thick silver necklace wedged between the cervical vertebrae, a decorative pin made of ivory and silver inlay, and a delicate hair clip fashioned from carved tortoiseshell.

"It wasn't no ghost," Hess said. "Sounded mechanical. I'm gonna go investigate."

Hunter Ivan jumped back slightly when he saw one of the two men he was photographing stand up, look around, and begin walking towards him.

Ivan was a forty-six-year-old man who lived by himself in Milwaukee, Wisconsin. Some called him a loner, and by his own admission, he probably was. Teased as a kid about his name and awkward stature, Hunter was simply never comfortable around people. Especially strangers. He was tall, nearly six foot seven, and his limbs were long and out of proportion, even for a man his height. He also had a severe case of acne as a teenager which left his thin face permanently scarred. Someone started calling him the "praying mantis" in high school and the name stuck. The few friends he had carried over from those days simply referred to him as *Mantis*. Hunter worked in a large brewery where he had been employed for nearly twenty years. He tried college for a while but dropped out after spending a year and a half at a state university in Wisconsin where he was majoring in engineering. He liked to tell people the math courses had killed him. But in reality, he just didn't see any use for college. He loved to read in his spare time, never planned on a family, and was content to work nine to five, using his annual two week vacation for an interesting trip. This year's adventure was a well planned solo kayak camping trip along the Wilderness Waterway from Flamingo to Everglades City.

Mantis was an advanced amateur photographer, who processed his own black and white film in a basement darkroom. He had brought along ten rolls of film for the one hundred-twelve mile trip.

As with all of his vacations, Mantis had worked out every detail months in advance, and he had packed the sixty pound kayak with over two hundred pounds of supplies including thirteen gallons of fresh water. Other items on his supply list included plenty of dried and canned food, a small one burner stove, a tent and sleeping bag, camera equipment, several books, toiletries, binoculars, a flashlight, spare batteries, and of course a compass and some waterproof navigation charts. Most people who attempted the Flamingo to Everglades route went by canoe, usually in a group of at least four people, and almost always during the winter months when the mosquitoes were at least tolerable. Mantis could only go on vacation during the July plant shutdown, so he just decided to make the best of the bug situation. In fact, he was happier this way since the chances of him running into other campers at the numerous Park Service campsites were small.

Mantis reached Pavilion Key on the eighth day of his trip. Thus far his vacation had been everything he could have hoped for. Solitude. Natural beauty. Genuine exercise. And plenty of things to take pictures of. He was scouting out Pavilion Key looking for birds to photograph when he spotted Baker and Hess digging in the sand. The only people Mantis had seen up to then were sport and commercial fisherman. So he decided to watch these guys for a while with his binoculars. When he saw what looked like a human skull come out of the hole they were digging, he pulled out his thirty-five millimeter Nikon with its four hundred millimeter zoom lens and began cranking off exposures with the help of a motor drive. He was already on his second roll of film when one of the men started heading towards him.

Mantis panicked at the sight of Neil Hess closing on his position. He turned and began to run through the thin layer of brush separating the east and west shores of the island. As soon as Mantis started into his loping gate, Hess caught site of him and began sprinting. Hearing Hess barreling through the sparse foliage to his rear, Mantis turned sharply to the left and began heading towards his kayak which was gently beached on the northeast shoreline about three-hundred yards away.

With Mantis weighted down with heavy photographic

equipment and binoculars, Hess was able to quickly close the gap between them, and by the time Mantis hit the open beach, Hess was just fifty yards behind. Without warning, Hess planted his feet, drew his .357 magnum revolver, and shot Mantis squarely in the left scapula. The impact of the heavily charged slug knocked Mantis to the ground like a daddy long-legs being flicked from a person's shoulder. Lying in the sand and moaning with pain, Mantis slid the camera and binoculars from around his neck and dropped them in the sand. He pawed at the wound in his back with his gangly right arm, struggled to his feet, and continued in a sort of zig-zag stagger towards his kayak.

Hess laughed to himself, knowing there was no escape for this nosy intruder, and fired off two more quick shots which passed cleanly beneath the flailing arms of Mantis. A fourth shot grazed the fleeing man's buttocks just as he reached the kayak. And the next two shots struck the small fiberglass vessel in the bow, just inches below Mantis's slumping body.

Hess was now out of ammunition and failed to carry any spare cartridges. Everything was back at the camp about a quarter mile south of his present location.

Mantis slowly pushed the loaded kayak into the shallow waters surrounding Pavilion Key's eastern shore, and with two painful strokes of the paddle, was clear of the beach and underlying shell-laden muck.

"Get the hell back here you bastard," Hess yelled. "I'm gonna kill you. Kill you, you hear!"

By this time Baker was on the eastern beach and heard Hess's threats. He also saw the kayak and its lanky occupant moving slowly away to the north and east.

"Get the Zodiac goddammit!" Hess yelled as he turned to face Baker who was now only a few yards away. "We gotta go after that guy. He was taking goddamn pictures of us!"

"You didn't shoot him, did ya?" Baker questioned in a surprised tone.

"Of course I shot him. Hit him twice, I think. Should have killed him too but I shot his damn boat instead."

"How bad's he hit?" Baker said. "I mean. Maybe he won't make it?"

"I don't know, you idiot. But he's still strong enough to paddle away from us. Shit, I wish I had some more damn bullets."

"Maybe we should just let him go? His camera and stuff are lyin' over there," Baker said, pointing to the place where Mantis had fallen. "And there's lots of blood."

"We're not letting him go. Now go get the Zodiac and meet me up at the point," Hess said gesturing to the northern most projection of Pavilion Key. "I'll keep an eye on him so he doesn't get away."

Mantis was hemorrhaging badly from the bullet wound in his back and was beginning to feel faint in the hot afternoon sun. The bullet had mushroomed when it hit his shoulder blade and one of the serrated edges from the jacketed slug had sliced through a major artery. The wound was mortal.

In his last conscious effort, Mantis pulled two exposed rolls of film from his pocket and stuffed them into one of the numerous dry compartments in the wall of the kayak. Then he made a few feeble attempts at paddling before slumping over in his fiberglass-encased seat like the collapsed superstructure on a sinking battleship. Mantis was dead.

Using the wounded man's discarded binoculars, Hess saw that the intruder had stopped paddling and didn't appear to be moving. *Maybe he had killed him after all?*

The whining of the Zodiac's outboard caught Hess's attention and he jerked around to see Baker motoring north along the western shore of Pavilion Key. When Baker reached the point of the island he slowly beached the inflatable craft, and waited patiently for Hess.

"Okay. Let's go get him," Hess panted, out of breath from his trek across the sand. "You drive."

"He don't look like he's movin'," Baker said as he reversed the outboard and turned towards the kayak. "Do ya think he's dead?"

"Might be. Might be faking," Hess said. "We'll soon see what this bastard's all about."

They reached the bobbing kayak in less than five minutes. The kayak rolled gently from side to side on the small afternoon waves like a toy in a child's bath.

"Poke him with the paddle," Hess said, sticking the aluminum emergency paddle in Baker's face. "If he moves, I'm shooting him."

But there was no movement from Mantis. Baker jostled him several times with the small oar. No response. "He sure looks like a goner, boss," Baker said at last.

"Yeah. I think you're right," Hess said as he stared coldly at the body. "Grab his boat so I can get a better look."

Baker wrapped his fingers around the padded edge of the paddler's compartment, careful not to touch the sticky pools of drying blood which seemed to be everywhere. "Okay. I got it," he said to Hess.

Hess heaved the dead man's torso backwards by pulling smartly on the collar of his shirt and Mantis sprawled face up on the rear of the kayak, slightly off center, causing the small vessel to list to port.

"Okay. He's dead," Hess said after seeing the lifeless eyes and gaping mouth which made Mantis look like a battered mannequin. "Now we gotta get rid of him."

Just then the sound of a full-throttle outboard could be heard in the distance, heading towards them from the southeast. The approaching boat's white bow-spray mustache was getting bigger every second and Hess developed a panicked look on his face. "Oh shit," he said. "What if that's a game warden? Or marine patrol? That sucker's really moving."

"What are we gonna do now?" Baker said anxiously.

"I'll tell you what we're gonna do. We'll sink the body," Hess said.

"Sink him?" Baker asked, perplexed.

"Yeah. Hide the evidence. Go untie the anchor. And hurry your ass."

Baker acted swiftly and untied the ten pound mushroom anchor from the line in the bow of the Zodiac. "Do you want any of the rope?" Baker asked.

"No. Too shallow for that. Just give me the damn anchor. And take a GPS reading of this spot."

Baker passed the freed anchor to Hess carefully. Like handing off a baby. Hess quickly went to work on Mantis, passing the dead man's leather belt through the eye of the anchor until everything was secure. Then he violently dragged the upper body of the dead man across the rear and side of the kayak and let gravity extricate Mantis's gangly legs from the hull of the small craft. In a matter of seconds Mantis was bubbling towards the shallow Florida Bay bottom. A mere four feet below Baker and Hess.

While Hess prepared Mantis for his aquatic grave, Baker recorded the GPS coordinates and scribbled them on a scrap of paper which he stuffed into his front pants pocket.

The approaching boat was only a half mile away and closing when they sunk Mantis. There was no time to do anything with the kayak so they turned and headed south, away from Pavilion Key, and into the Gulf of Mexico.

"That kayak's drifting pretty good in the moving tide," Hess said. When that boat reaches it they'll never find the body. Might not even know there ever *was* a body."

"But boss. What about all that blood?" It's all over the dang boat," Baker shouted over the fast moving air that was swallowing their speeding Zodiac. "And they probably saw us floatin' next to the damn thing."

"Don't worry about it. By the time they tow that fancy canoe back to Chokoloskee and figure out there was a body attached to it, we'll be long gone. No one will ever find us. And even if they do. No body. No murder."

But the westbound speedboat didn't stop for the kayak. Didn't even slow down for that matter. The kayak had continued to ride the incoming tide towards shore, and the speedboat, which turned out to be a guided flats fishing boat with impatient clients aboard, whizzed by about two hundred yards south of the abandoned kayak.

Baker and Hess were already bouncing off some of the Gulf of Mexico chop, nearly a mile south of Pavilion Key. With the aid of their scavenged binoculars, they were able to see that the speedboat hadn't stopped for the kayak.

"Maybe we should go back and get it," Baker shouted to Hess.

"No way. What if the guy turns around? Or what if another boat comes along?" Hess said. "We're gonna go 'bout another mile and wait things out 'til it gets dark. Then head back to camp. We'll go looking for the dead guy's boat in the morning."

FIFTEEN

"THESE BASTARDS OUGHT TO BE HATCHING BY NOW," Applegate said quietly to himself. "Something should have happened already." Dean Applegate's patience had run thinner than the hair on a beached coconut, and he decided to open one of the sea turtle eggs in his garage.

He didn't want to be disturbed, so he waited until Susan had taken the kids to the mall in Naples where they were going to meet some of their friends and go to a matinee while she did some shopping. He knew he had a nice window of time to quietly tinker with his incubating charges.

Applegate randomly selected one of the five gallon buckets and gently scraped away the upper layer of sand with a small trowel until the first white egg appeared, looking like a golf ball stuck in a moist sand trap. He removed the egg with the forefinger and thumb of his right hand, and proceeded to dust the clinging sand grains from the egg with his free hand. Now the egg was clean. With the egg wedged into the palm of his left hand, he stabbed the scissors of his Swiss army knife into the leathery shell. A trickle of albumin flowed quickly from the puncture site and began to fill the thin cracks in his hand. He stared at the violated egg for a minute, then made several quick slices with the scissors, nearly cleaving the egg in two. The egg was now opened up in his palm like a bisected baked potato. And it contained only albumin and some off-color yolk.

"Dammit," he said in a quick, audible tone. "It's a goddamn dud." Then he heaved the infertile egg against the wall of the garage, wiped his hand across his pant leg, and knelt down to pick up another egg. The second one was also infertile. By the time he unearthed the third egg he had become very edgy, bordering on panicky, and his mind began to race with thoughts of an incubator full of duds and no hatchlings to sell in Miami. As he ripped through the third egg with his sticky scissors, a small, almost fully formed turtle slipped through his fingers and fell with a plop to the concrete garage floor. Applegate watched from above as it moved its little flippers slowly forward and backward. The head rolled slightly to the left. Then to the right. And then, after only about a minute, there was no movement at all. The turtle was dead.

Applegate bent over, picked up the moist embryo, and noted that there was still quite a bit of yolk attached to the turtle's umbilical area. The turtle was probably at least two weeks premature. So his calculations had been slightly off. And worst of all, if only one in three of his eggs were viable, he'd have only twenty-four hatchlings to sell to Greene. And the Miami quota was fifty! He mulled this over for a while and realized his only course of action. Return to Pavilion Key and dig up another nest. He needed more eggs.

And he still had almost four hours before Susan and the kids would be home.

Plenty of time if he moved quickly.

Jasper Wiley hurried on his seventy-five year-old legs from the screened dining area of the Rod & Gun Club to the 1960s style black telephone which squatted firmly on the reception desk.

"Hal. Jasper here. You said to call if I saw anythin' suspicious," Wiley said slowly into the mouthpiece, making sure he correctly pronounced all of the syllables in suspicious. "Well. Dean Applegate just went past the Club and is headed south on the Barron towards the channel. And I didn't see any fishin' equipment aboard. What should I do?"

"Just sit tight old friend. And make a notation of the time. Both going and coming," Hal replied from his office in the ranger station. "If he's headed to Pavilion, he should be back in a few hours."

"Okay. But shouldn't we trail him?" Jasper pleaded. "Maybe we could catch him in the act or somethin'?"

"Too late already," Hal said. "Time I get over there and we get on the water, he's already on Pavilion. If that's where he's going. And if he sees us approaching, he's likely to dump any evidence. Nope. Patience is the key. If he's doing something illegal, we'll catch up with him later."

"All right Hal," Jasper exhaled. "Whatever you say. I'll write down the times."

"I don't see shit," Neil Hess barked from his position in the bow of the Zodiac. Are you looking, Baker?"

"Yeah I'm lookin', boss," Baker replied. "But I don't

see nothin' neither. It's like the thing just turned invisible. But what I *do* see is a boat headin' kinda towards us."

Baker and Hess had been up since daybreak searching the shore of Pavilion Key and the surrounding mangrove-coated islets for Mantis's small craft. But the kayak was nowhere to be found.

When Baker noticed Dean Applegate approaching from the northwest, he and Hess were in Duck Rock Cove, a shallow bay of a place tucked between Duck Rock and the mainland's mangrove thickets. About a mile due north of Pavilion Key.

"That boat's heading for Pavilion," Hess said anxiously.

"How d'ya know that?" Baker said.

"He's skirting the north side of Little Pavilion, you idiot," Hess said visciously. "Nobody does that less they're heading to the Chatham River. And that ain't no flats boat. Give me them damn binoculars. And cut the engine so I can see."

Baker handed Hess Mantis's binoculars which he had stashed in the back of the Zodiac.

"Well shoot me full a holes," Hess exclaimed. "It looks like our Fish and Wildlife friend. You still got the numbers from his boat?"

"Course I do, boss," Baker replied proudly. "Got 'em tucked right here in my wallet."

With the help of Hess's abrasive directions, Baker paddled the Zodiac into a crook of mangroves where the two thieves were well hidden, but could still observe the western shore of Pavilion Key. Mantis's high quality binoculars couldn't retrieve the approaching boat's bow registration numbers, but the skimming boat certainly looked like the turtle egg collector's vessel Baker and Hess had seen over a month ago.

"These bugs suck," Baker whined as he swatted wildly at the air around him in an effort to ward off the persistent mosquito squadron. "Can't we get outta here?"

"If I gotta shoot you to shut you up I will you candy-ass," Hess snapped back. "We're not moving an inch 'til Ranger Rick hits the beach."

Applegate expertly slid his Carolina Skiff along the hot Pavilion Key sand like an iron moving smoothly over a piece of delicate fabric. Then he tossed the anchor high on the beach, grabbed a shovel and two plastic five gallon buckets, and headed south along the western shore of the island at a brisk pace.

By now Baker had the Zodiac fired up, and with the wind blowing at close to fifteen knots from the south, there was no way Applegate would hear them coming. Ten minutes later they were pulling the Zodiac over the mucky bottom of Pavilion Key's eastern tidal lagoon. After securing the air-filled craft, they clamored through the palmettos and scratchy prickly-pears until they had a foliage-obstructed view of the western shoreline.

"There he is, boss," Baker muttered. "He's hangin' round the grave site."

"Hey. We don't know for sure it's a grave site," Hess answered sharply. Then he added, "wonder what the hell he's doing?"

Applegate was more than surprised when about one hundred yards north of the ridley nesting area he noticed a patch of freshly disturbed sand and numerous recently created footprints. The spot was certainly high enough on the beach for a sea turtle nest, but who else knew about the

116

Pavilion ridleys? Or was he just being paranoid? Maybe some campers had built a fire on the beach and snuffed it out with shoveled sand. Applegate inverted his shovel and pressed hard on the bumpy sand with the blunt wooden handle.

"You gonna shoot 'im, boss?" Baker whispered to Hess, who didn't have his revolver drawn.

"No. I ain't gonna shoot him you dope. He ain't gonna find nothing less he starts digging. We covered them bones up real good."

"Then what's he doin' with the shovel? Backwards and all," Baker questioned.

"Probably checking to see if it's a turtle nest. If the ground's hollow there," Hess said.

And Neil Hess was correct. Applegate spent about fifteen minutes poking the sand in and around the footprints, probing for the tell-tale cavity of a sea turtle nest. Convinced that there were no nests in the immediate vicinity, and that the roughened footprint-strewn sand could have been produced by a dozen scenarios, he lumbered on towards the ridley nesting area.

Baker and Hess watched Applegate intently, like hyenas, cowardly but dangerous, waiting for the right moment to fall upon vulnerable prey. In a short while, Applegate was surveying the beach spot where he had exhumed the three buckets of eggs and sand weeks earlier. After a brief foray into the inland brush, he returned to the beach with what appeared to be a thin, straight, piece of wood. This sloughed appendage from a nearby gumbo limbo would function as his nest probing tool.

"Looks like he's goin' for more of them turtle eggs," Baker said, just a little too loud for Hess's liking.

"Will you keep it down. Moron!" Hess whisper-shouted. "We don't need him spotting us 'til I want him to spot us."

"Looks like he found somethin'," Baker said with a hush, not budging the rubberized oculars of the field glasses from his eye sockets. "That stick is stuck far down. And he's pawin' at the sand pretty good with his hands."

A few minutes of silence passed before Baker jumped a little and said, "He's grabbin' the shovel. He's startin' to dig."

Applegate uncovered the top layer of eggs after about ten minutes of steady but gentle excavating. Then he dropped the shovel, fell easily to his knees, and reached into the hole, pulling out three sand-speckled eggs with one grab.

"Time to move in a little closer," Hess whispered. "I wanna see exactly what's goin' on over there."

Baker and Hess crept through the sparse foliage separating themselves from Applegate, and stopped a mere fifty feet away. Hess grabbed the binoculars from Baker and stuck them to his head just in time to witness a squirming, near-term Kemp's ridley embryo being torn from its protective capsule by Dean Applegate's bulky fingers. Further inspection by Hess revealed that this was the third egg Applegate had ripped open. Three embryos lay on the sizzling Pavilion Key sand at Applegate's feet.

"Okay. We go," Hess said. Baker looked up at his partner with surprise and his already contracted eyelids pulled back a little more when he noticed that Hess was palming his revolver—with the hammer pulled back.

Applegate, off duty, had a snub-nosed .38 special concealed in a small leather holster tucked inside the

118

beltline of his pants. But he never even had the chance to grab for it.

"Reach for the clouds, asshole," Hess yelled as he came crashing through the brush, gun first, followed closely by Baker. "Or you're a killed man."

In one continuous action, Applegate dropped the torn and empty egg shell, raised his albumin and mucus coated hands in the air, and uncontrollably defecated in his pants.

"Bobby. I think we scared the piss outta this jerk-off," Hess said, pointing the revolver towards the expanding urine stain forming around the fly of Applegate's trousers. "What's your name, jerk-off?"

The reality of what was happening had started to filter through the frightened haze in Applegate's head.

"Do I gotta shoot you, egg man?" Hess growled. "What's your damn name?"

Applegate had dealt with killers before. And he knew a killer by his eyes. They had a special kind of mean glare. The man yelling at him and waving the revolver had a killer's eyes.

"Dean," Applegate replied. "My name is Dean."

"Go grab his wallet," Hess said to Baker without taking his eyes or the Colt off of Applegate. Baker walked over to the tall, odorous man, and gingerly reached into Applegate's back right pants pocket and retrieved the wallet like a store clerk carefully removing a piece of fine jewelry from a display cabinet.

"Now bring it here and open it up," Hess said. "See if you can find his driver's license."

Baker, as usual, followed Hess's directions closely, and after fumbling with the snake skin wallet for a minute, produced a Florida driver's license. "Got it!" he said with a big grin.

"What's it say?" Hess barked impatiently.

"Says. . . . State of Flor-i-da Di-vi-sion of Mo-tor Ve-hic—"

"Not that, you idiot! What's his goddamn name?!"

"Oh. Sorry boss," Baker said softly. "Dean Apple-gate. Lives in Naples."

"Anything else in there look important?" Hess said.

"Well. Here's some kinda official ID card. Got a gold seal on it," Baker said as he rotated the plastic card from front to back like a bouncer checking a college kid's identification. Then a surprised Baker said, "he's a dang U.S. Fish and Wildlife Officer."

"So he *is* a Ranger Rick," Hess said with a sinister smile to Baker. "Well, how 'bout if officer Applegate throws his weapon on the ground before I shoot off his head." Then, looking straight at Applegate, he added, "use your left hand. And move real slow."

Applegate quickly considered the close range and cocked hammer of his adversary's revolver, and wisely extracted his snubnose, still in its holster, and dropped it on the beach where it landed with a soft, sandy splash.

"Go get the gun, Bobby," Hess said. "And feel him up real good. All over. For any other hardware."

Baker thoroughly frisked Applegate. And finding nothing but some keys and a pocket knife, picked up the officer's gun from the sand and returned to Hess's side.

"Now that we got the formalities outta the way," Hess said, relaxing his grip on the revolver and converting it back to double action with his thumb. "Why don't you tell us what you're doing out here on Pavilion with these turtle eggs?"

Applegate's impulse was to return the question with a question of his own. But he didn't want to push this snarly killer, so he opted to lie instead.

"Do you even need to ask such a question?" Applegate said, his voice wavering just a little. "I'm doing a sea turtle nesting survey. Part of a federal program designed to monitor—"

The sharp pain and fire-like burning produced as the bullet passed through Applegate's right calf muscle stopped him mid-sentence. His eyes remained fixed on Hess and the smoking revolver as he instinctively reached for the wound in his leg.

"Okay. You don't gotta lie to us, Officer Applegate," Hess said, content with his non-fatal handiwork. "We may look a little rough, but we ain't stupid. This ain't the first time we've seen you sneaking around out here on Pavilion in plain clothes. So if you want to see another sunset, you better give us the straight skinny from now on."

Applegate winced in pain as he examined his blood-covered right hand. "All right. Shit. You shot me," he said between his teeth. Then he stuck his hand back on his leaking leg and, looking up at Hess, said, "mind if I sit down?"

"Sure. Make yourself comfortable," Hess said sarcastically. "Grab some ass-sand. But remember, your legs are a smaller target if you do. So I wouldn't advise lyin' to me again."

Applegate sat down Indian-style and was able to steal a better look at the fresh bullet wound in his leg. The slug had gone cleanly through his calf, about an inch deep to the skin, and a large blood clot was beginning to form within and around the wound. Despite the intense pain, Applegate was relieved that the tibia and fibula appeared to have been spared, he could move his toes, and there was no sign of arterial bleeding.

"Here's the story," Applegate began, removing a hand-kerchief from his front pants pocket and using his belt to apply a makeshift pressure bandage to the leg. He spoke continuously to Hess and Baker for about ten minutes. He told them of the Kemp's ridley, including a brief natural history review—of how he stumbled upon the nesting site on a weekend fishing trip—and his plans to sell the hatch-lings to an animal dealer in Miami. Not wanting to risk another bullet wound from the psycho—Applegate even included the details of how much he'd be paid for each hatchling—and the fact that he already had eggs incubat-ing at home in his garage.

"So why d'ya come back to Pavilion if you already got enough eggs at home?" Hess asked, obviously intrigued by Applegate's tale.

"Had some duds. They weren't all going to hatch."

Hess grabbed his chin with his left hand and pressed his cheeks against his teeth while staring at the ground where the dead embryos lay. "So you're back for more ba-bies. And looks like these new eggs got turtles in 'em."

"Yes. Well, you can see that plain as I can," Applegate said following Hess's eye-path to the sand. "Listen. There's plenty of hatchlings now. Maybe we can work out some sort of deal?"

Hess looked over to Baker and smiled broadly like a cartoon character with a brilliant idea. "Hear that Bobby? Ranger Rick wants to make a deal. What do you think? Is he worth it?"

Baker, realizing Hess expected a response, tried to scrape up some intelligent words from the thin brain film containing his vocabulary. "Well, boss. I dunno. I mean.

We can dig up them eggs as good as he can. And take 'em to Miami to sell. Maybe we could just get rid of 'im. He could finger us, ya know."

Applegate squirmed uneasily in the sand at Baker's comments. His impulse was to shout out that without him, they'd have little or no chance at hatching the turtles—much less marketing them—but he elected to keep quiet and see what the psycho had to say.

Hess just looked at Baker and shook his head back and forth. "Bobby. Bobby. It's a good thing I'm in charge here. See. We're gonna *need* Ranger Rick's connections. Plus, we'll let him do all the dirty work and we'll collect the money. Not all of it of course. We'll let him keep a third—which is pretty fair since there are three of us in this partnership." Then Hess turned to Applegate. "Sound fair to you, partner?"

Applegate was jammed in tight. Like a wood screw in a hole. The money no longer seemed so important—he was just hoping to get off of Pavilion Key with his life. "Sounds fair. I think we can do this thing. But would you mind putting the gun away? You won't need to shoot me again."

Hess stuffed the revolver back into his pants and, addressing Baker, said, "go help our partner to his feet. We've got some digging to do."

Under Applegate's supervision, Baker removed the remaining seventy-two eggs from the already opened nest and eighty-six eggs from a second cache' that they located about ten yards from the first.

As Baker and Hess carried the egg buckets towards Applegate's boat with the limping Wildlife Officer in the lead, Hess said with a chuckle, "now I don't feel so bad collecting all that money, 'cause lugging these buckets around is hard work."

When the threesome reached the Carolina Skiff, the buckets were carefully loaded aboard and Applegate gingerly got behind the center console controls. Then Hess said, "smile Ranger Rick," as he pulled a disposable camera from his back pocket and made several exposures of Applegate with the egg buckets in plain view. Hess had also photographed Applegate directing Baker during the nest excavation. "That's just a little insurance policy in case you get any ideas of bagging out on this whole thing."

"You won't need those pictures. I'll follow through," Applegate said.

"That's a hundred-thirty-three thousand for the first fifty babies—two thirds of fifty times four thousand dollars—and if you sell anymore, we get two thirds of what your guy pays you," Hess said.

"But. They won't all hatch! They *never* all hatch," Applegate said, exasperated. "And some of the ones that do die because they're too weak. What if we don't get fifty good ones, even with all of these new eggs?"

"Well, now," Hess said sarcastically. "You're the one playin' turtle mommy. So that's gonna be *your* problem. A hundred-thirty-five thousand. I decided to round up a little. We'll be in touch."

Applegate had a lot to think about on the ride back to Everglades City. The most pressing problem being how to explain the now throbbing leg wound to his wife and co-workers.

SIXTEEN

D<small>EAN</small> A<small>PPLEGATE</small> <small>MOVED WITH AN OBVIOUS LIMP AS HE</small> shuttled gear from the Skiff to his pickup at the boat landing—like a lame feral cat moving her kittens from one hiding place to the next. It was nearly three o'clock in the afternoon—the sun was still high—and the muggy air made Applegate feel as though he was working out in a sauna.

Jasper watched with interest as Applegate loaded the last white bucket into the pickup and hobbled back to check the trailer connections. It was then that Jasper noticed the bloodstained makeshift bandage on Applegate's leg.

When Applegate drove away to the north, Jasper scurried back to the Rod & Gun Club and phoned Hal. "He's back," Jasper said before Hal even knew who was on the other end of the line. "He just loaded up and is headin' north on twenty-nine. Are you gonna go after him?"

"Settle down, Jasper," Hal said in a calm tone. "We're in no hurry here. If he's doing something illegal, we'll get it sorted out. Just keep your eyes open. You're doing great."

By the time Applegate pulled into his driveway, he had his story for Susan and the kids pretty straight. While they were away at the mall, he got the fishing bug and decided to go out in the Back Country for some redfish and snook. Everything was going well—he was even catching some nice ones—when the urge to relieve himself in a manner that couldn't be dealt with over the gunwale came upon him. So he headed for the nearest landfall—Pavilion Key—and while he was making his way over the beach in the direction of the Port-O-John, he tripped and caught his leg fast on an old iron spike jutting from a weathered six by six.

"You outta get a tetanus shot, honey," Susan said upon hearing the story. "Let me take a look at it. I'll clean it up for you."

"No need for that," Applegate replied, unconsciously retrieving the injured limb. "I'm fine. I'll take care of it. And see a doctor on Monday if it makes you feel any better."

Susan knew better than to challenge her stubborn husband. She just hoped he would follow through with the doctor visit.

After Applegate settled the new eggs into the turtle nursery, he locked himself in the bathroom and set about cleaning the pulsing wound. He flushed the hole as best he could with some warm tap water and followed that with peroxide—which bubbled and gurgled in the pulpy cavity like a child's science project. Then he packed the wound with half a tube of triple antibiotic ointment, covered it with an extra large Band-Aid, and limped downstairs for the dinner which Susan was busy preparing.

"We won't be needing this stupid thing anymore," Neil Hess said as he kicked at the metal detector which lay on the ground of their campsite. "And to think—all we really would have needed was a sharp stick to find the real treasure on this poor excuse for an island."

"Ya sure about this turtle plan, boss?" Baker said. "I mean. Ya sure his whole story about sellin' these little turtles for lots of money is true?"

"Oh, it's true," Hess said confidently. "You can bet it's the real deal, Bobby boy. We're sittin' pretty right now—just gotta hope the guy can hatch the damn things. Only thing is—we have to hole up here on this baking strip of dirt until he shows up with the cash. And from what he says—and I believe him—it could be another couple weeks. Maybe more."

"Boss. You know how this place is gettin' to me," Baker said in a submissive tone. "Maybe I could head back to Miami—or someplace—and wait there. 'Specially since we ain't doin' no more treasure huntin'."

"Bobby. Bobby," Hess said with a tilted grin. "We're a team. You and me. Sorry. No trips to the mainland for you. Wouldn't want you payin' a visit to Ranger Rick."

"C'mon, boss. I wouldn't do that," Baker said sincerely. "It's just the bugs and the heat. I need some AC."

"In fact," Hess added, ignoring Baker's last comment. "I'll be the one going into town for supplies from now on."

"Well, you better think about makin' a trip soon then. 'Cause we're almost outta fresh water and ice."

"Okay—no problem. I'll go into Chokoloskee first thing in the morning. But right now I'm gonna have me a little nap. And dream of little turtles turnin' into dollar signs."

Hal had trouble sleeping the night of Jasper's most recent phone call—turning in bed like a piece of thick grill chicken that just won't cook through. Maybe he should've tailed Applegate. Maybe he *was* being too conservative with the whole Pavilion Key situation? Perhaps it *was* time for another trip out there? Once he'd finally made up his mind to go visit the island again, he settled into what could best be described as half-sleep.

By seven the next morning Hal had showered, dressed, and called Jasper at the Club.

"Can you spare a few hours, Jasper?" Hal asked politely. "I've been doing some thinking; we outta go out and see what's happening on Pavilion."

"Ready anytime, Hal," Jasper replied enthusiastically. "You pickin' me up?"

"Yeah. Meet me at the public landing in twenty minutes. This shouldn't take long."

"I got all day, Hal. It's Sunday—remember?"

"Of course. Forgot you were a nine-to-fiver."

Ignoring Hal's humor, Jasper added, "Are you bringin' Lydia along—I mean—is she uh—"

"No. She's not here this weekend," Hal said cutting Jasper off. Despite Hal's attempts at secrecy, Jasper and a few others knew of his romance with Lydia. "She's doing some research stuff up in Melbourne for a few days, but she might be down for a visit next weekend."

"Okay. Well, see you in a few," the smiling Jasper said before hanging up the phone.

Bobby Baker was surprised to hear the whine of the approaching outboard so soon—Hess had only been gone about an hour—barely enough time to get to Chokoloskee and back without stopping. His surprise morphed into concern when he realized that the closing craft was not their Zodiac, but a Florida Game and Fresh Water Fish patrol boat. *What should he do? What would Hess do? What would Hess want him to do? Shit. A lot had happened out here over the past few days. Whatever he decided would probably be wrong—at least in Hess's eyes—and he'd get in trouble.* So he elected to do nothing at all, except watch and see what happened next.

Two men got out of the boat and secured it to the beach. The same two Baker and Hess had seen about a month ago. But this time there was no woman with them. *Why did they have to come now—when the boss was away? He'd know what to do; take care of 'em like he took care of that Ranger Rick guy.*

"I knew something was goin' on," Jasper said as he and Hal examined the open nest. Their attention was quickly drawn to the scattered egg shells and three dried Kemp's ridley embryos on the sand. "Still think someone's takin' eggs to eat, Hal?"

Hal was on his knees, holding the three little turtle chips in the palm of his right hand. Jasper began to scavenge the curly egg shell fragments. "I really don't know what to think, Jasper. It doesn't make any sense. If you *want* eggs. Then *take* eggs. If you want turtles. Then either take the eggs—or wait here for them to hatch and take 'em alive."

"That's it, Hal," Jasper said with a nod. "I think I understand what's happenin'."

"Okay. I'm all ears."

"Well. Let's just say someone wants a bunch of baby sea turtles. For whatever reason," Jasper said.

"Yeah."

"All right. So that person doesn't have time to hang out on the beach and wait for the little buggers to crawl out of the sand—but he *could* bring 'em—the eggs that is—

home, and hatch 'em there. And if it's Applegate doin' the diggin'—he probably has the eggs stashed somewhere safe."

"Could be, Jasper. I follow your logic. Except how do you explain these dead ones?"

"Don't got that figured out yet," Jasper said optimistically. But give me a chance—I ain't as sharp as I used to be, but I'll get it."

"Unless," Hal said thoughtfully. "He's staging them."

"Staging? What d'ya mean by staging?"

"You know. Seeing how far they are along. When they're likely to hatch."

"But why do that here on the beach? It wastes time. And increases the chance of gettin' found out."

"Well . . . but what if the eggs were duds. Infertile," Hal said. "If you're idea is correct—and the person doing this wants *live* turtles—then lugging a bunch of sterile eggs back to the mainland would be a real risky waste of time."

"Hmmm," Jasper nodded. "Didn't think of it that way."

Hal pulled his compact Olympus thirty-five millimeter camera from his pocket and snapped a few quick pictures of the nest site. Then, with Jasper's help, he placed the dried hatchlings and their shells into a small plastic sandwich baggie and the two men headed back toward their boat.

Baker watched as the Game and Fish boat slipped from the beach, turned, and headed away from Pavilion Key to the north and west.

Boy, did he have some stuff to tell the boss when he got back from Chokoloskee.

130

SEVENTEEN

THE SHARP STAINLESS STEEL BLADE PAUSED FOR A MOMENT when it struck metal, then, with the force provided by the meaty hand directing it, the knife continued through the thick stomach wall and surrounding viscera before it found light again at the base of the throat. The knife handler then put the blade down, inverted the body, and tugged firmly on the pendulous guts until they plopped on the plexiglass cleaning table with a viscous thud. Curious as to what type of object had detoured his cutting stroke, the fisherman poked at the entrails with a bloody finger and was quite surprised to find a man's ring laying across the crop-like folds of the fish stomach's lining. Wiping the bulky ring on his pants, the fisherman was able to make out the words, "Fifteen Years—Komen Brewery," which circled a light green gem in the center of the ring. Engraved on the inside was the inscription, "H.I. 1993."

"Hey! Jim found a dang ring in that big catfish," the fish cleaner's friend yelled to a couple of other guys who were loading up a minivan with fishing gear and coolers.

"You gotta check this out. A big *gold* ring. Sittin' right in the belly of this here fish."

The other two fishing buddies dropped what they were doing and headed over to the fish cleaning station which consisted of a large wooden table, a freshwater hose, and a few well placed drain holes. The entire structure was bolted to the edge of the Chokoloskee Marina dock so that fish body parts could be dropped or tossed effortlessly to patient crabs and hovering gulls. By the time the two friends joined the rest of their party at the dock, a small crowd of people, tourists mostly, had descended upon the fish cleaner. Sure enough they all marveled, a ring had indeed been found in the stomach of a catfish. What were the chances some of them muttered? Almost nobody kept catfish, and those few that did rarely cleaned them. Considered "trash fish," they usually just ended up as fertilizer in the garden.

Randy Wells was the National Marine Fisheries Service agent assigned to dock duty that day. Twenty-four years old and recently minted from the University of Miami with a degree in fisheries management, Wells's clean-cut good looks and middle school-smooth face made him anything but intimidating. And this was okay since his job didn't require intimidation or conflict. He was merely a survey taker—didn't even check licenses—that stuff was up to law enforcement. His job was to ask the fisherman some demographic questions, what he or she had caught, where they caught it, and whether they kept the fish or not. Pretty routine information most days. Noticing the commotion at the cleaning station, he broke off his conversation with an awkwardly friendly but scruffy and weathered fellow in a Zodiac pontoon boat, and walked slowly towards the crowd gathering on the dock.

"Somebody catch a big one?" Wells said in a loud voice, straining on his tip toes and bobbing from side to side to see through the crowd which now consisted of about a dozen people.

"Some guy found a ring in a fish," a woman shouted. "And it looks like gold. With a big stone too!"

"Ring in a fish, huh?" Wells said matter-of-factly. "Mind if I slip in there and have a look?"

Wells easily made his way to the edge of the cleaning station where a large middle-aged man wearing cutoff jeans and a dirt and fish blood stained t-shirt stood. The man had a big grin on his face and was playfully trying to stuff the ring onto his pinky finger to the delight of his friends.

"Mind if I ask you a few questions about your fishing trip?" Wells said to the man in a friendly tone.

The fisherman just laughed. "No sir. Ask away. I never had a trip quite like this one."

Wells learned that the man and his friends were from Fort Lauderdale and that this was their first trip into the Back Country. They had rented a sixteen-foot aluminum jonboat with a twenty-five horsepower Mercury outboard, standard issue at the Chokoloskee marina, and burned up almost two full six-gallon tanks of gasoline on their trip which took them to the mouth of the Chatham river and back.

"We were goin' for redfish and trout. You know, to eat," the beaming fisherman said. "But we didn't get any. Just five of these topsail cats and a couple flounder. And two big snook—which we threw back of course—knowin' they're not in season."

"Well it's good to know you've read the rule book," Wells said sincerely, impressed that these weekend meat hunters hadn't poached any snook. "Mind if I take a look at your new ring?"

"Pretty weird, huh?" The fisherman said as he handed the now shiny men's ring to Wells. "I mean. Where would a fish get hold of something like this?"

"I really can't say," Wells said slowly as he twirled the ring between his fingers like a pawn shop owner. "But I can tell you this. It wasn't in your fish very long."

"How d'ya know that?" one of the fisherman's friends asked.

"A catfish will eat almost anything. Especially something that might reflect light like a piece of jewelry. This ring for instance," Wells said confidently as he readily drew upon information he acquired in his college ichthyology courses. "And they've got a large mouth and equally large esophagus. So they can eat big stuff. But they're also real good at regurgitating things that they can't digest. Rocks. Clam shells. Stuff like that. Those kinds of things sit in the sac-like stomach for a few days, maybe a week, and then the fish just barfs 'em up. That's what should have happened to your ring. So I'm guessing the fish ate it within the past week. You're pretty lucky."

"Oh. It probably ain't worth much," the man said smiling, politely taking the ring back from Wells. "But it sure makes a great story. And hell. I might even try to find the owner."

"Boy would that guy be surprised," Wells said. "When that ring went into the water I'm sure he never thought it would be found. By the way. Where did you catch that catfish?"

"Well I can't be sure. We got a little lost out there," the fisherman said sheepishly. "But I think we weren't far from a pretty big island. Called something like Picnic Key."

"Picnic Key?" Wells asked, familiar with the Ten Thousand Islands but never hearing of a Picnic Key. "You must mean Pavilion Key?"

"Yeah! That sounds right. Like I said, we didn't always know where we was out there, but that Pavilion Key was good size and seemed to fit with what we had on the chart they gave us in the rental office."

Wells made a final notation on the survey form, bid the group at the cleaning station good day, and headed towards a guided flats boat that was just pulling into the marina. He also noted that the scruffy guy in the Zodiac was no longer around.

Neil Hess cut the engine and let the Zodiac glide into Baker's waiting hands. "Bobby. Do you remember if that skinny guy with the camera was wearing a ring?" Hess said as he jumped from the Zodiac. The two men then began tugging on the light craft, lifting it onto the beach towards high ground.

"I gotta tell ya somethin', boss," Baker said, ignoring Hess completely. "While you was—"

"I asked you a damn question, boy!" Hess shouted. "Did the dead kayak guy have a ring on any of his fingers?!"

"Uh. . . . I don't remember, boss," Baker replied quietly, wondering what this had to do with *anything*.

"Well I don't either," Hess said angrily. "Can't even recall what his hands *looked* like."

Baker was confused. "Why you askin', boss?"

"Aw it's probably nothin'. Some fisherman found a ring in a fish he caught, and I remember seeing one of them Chokoloskee rentals circling close to the island real early this mornin'."

Baker tried to suppress a snicker. "So you think maybe this guy caught a fish that ate part of the dead guy on the bottom and—"

"Forget it," Hess snapped, cutting Baker off again. "Guess I'm just a little jittery, that's all. Now what do you got to tell me?"

"The game warden and the old guy were back while you was away. Ya know, the one's we saw a few weeks back checkin' out the beach. But this time there was no girl," Baker said with a slight cringe.

Hess said nothing. He simply nodded and began hauling the supplies from the Zodiac over to the campsite. Baker grabbed two bags of groceries and followed slowly behind, carefully dodging prickly pears and wild yuccas like a soldier moving deftly through a mine field. But he kept his distance. Neil Hess was worried and upset. A bad combination in Baker's experience.

"And I thought *I* had an exciting job," Hal chuckled to Randy Wells between sips of coffee. "A catfish coughing up jewelry. And you were there to see it! Man. I thought all you fisheries guys did was weigh gonads and count scale rings."

"C'mon, Hal. We get to *measure* fish sometimes. . . . and even ID the occasional oddball," Wells replied sarcastically. "A ring in a fish's belly is all in a day's work."

Hal and Randy were good friends. Had been for several years. They met as teammates playing men's softball, and although neither played much anymore, they would occasionally hit the links for a round of golf or do a little bowling in town. They also liked to have breakfast together a couple times a month at Jane's Restaurant in Ochopee, where they mostly shared job related stories.

Both still bachelors, they also talked a lot about women and their current relationships. After a few more minutes of playful wisecracks about Randy's occupation, Wells turned the conversation to the topic of Hal's relationship with Lydia Phillon.

They talked about Lydia until Hal felt they had exhausted the subject. He liked thinking about Lydia a lot more than he liked talking about her. "Well, I gotta get going. I have an especially urgent call to make this morning."

"Not going to propose over the phone, are you?" Wells kidded.

"Hey. Things are going well. But we're a long way from that," Hal said as he stood up and swiped the check from the tilted table. "I'll get it today."

"Well thanks," Wells said as he followed Hal to the register. "I'll get you next time."

Hal glanced at his watch when he got into the steamy Blazer. Eight forty-five. Shifting the vehicle quickly into drive, he hurtled out of the gravel parking lot and headed west towards the Ranger station. He wanted to get Applegate on the phone before the federal wildlife officer became distracted with the day's workload. Most of those feds up at the Naples I-75 tollbooth office started work promptly at nine.

Hal ran the conversation over in his mind several times like a school kid getting up the nerve to ask a girl out on a date. *How could he make this call without implying that Applegate was guilty of something? On the other hand, he didn't want to spook Applegate if something really was going on.* It would be tricky, but there was no way around the call. It was the best way to feel Applegate out. And much less formal or threatening than a personal visit.

Dean Applegate silenced the beeping phone by quickly grabbing the receiver. "Applegate here," the gruff voice said after Hal had waited a few seconds for the call to be transferred from the secretary's desk.

"Officer Applegate. This is Hal Noble over at Game and Fish. We've met a couple times."

"Yeah. Sure. The woodpecker guy," Applegate replied lightly. "What can I do for you?"

"Well. I'd like to ask you a few questions about some stuff that's been going on out at Pavilion Key," Hal said with a quick swallow at the end of the sentence.

"Pavilion Key?" Applegate replied after a pause that was just a half second too long. "You mean Pavilion Key the island? Way down past Chokoloskee?"

"That's the one," Hal replied. "There's been some weird beach activity down there lately. What looks like excavated sea turtle nests. Even some dead hatchlings."

"So what's unusual about that?" Applegate replied just slightly defensively. "I mean, all kinds of things happen to sea turtle nests. Like coons digging them up. Or high surf washing them out. I guess I wouldn't call a few dug up turtle nests *weird*."

"Yeah, I know. It does sound a little crazy," Hal said apologetically. "But there's a pattern to it. And some evidence that a person or people might be involved. I know you do some fishing out that way. Just wondering if you've seen anything suspicious." Then he added, "I'm sort of calling around to see if anyone can help me out."

"Wish I could. But I don't pay much attention to the beaches when I'm fishing the Back Country," Applegate said in a calm, almost rehearsed tone. "In fact, I was just out that way this weekend. Even stopped on Pavilion for a potty break. But didn't notice anything along my walk to the Park Service Port-O-John. And when I say didn't notice

138

anything, I mean it. Tripped over a piece of old timber that had a rusty spike in it. Took a pretty good cut to the leg."

"Sorry to hear that," Hal said, impressed with how direct Applegate was. Maybe the guy *was* on the level. Maybe he and Jasper had gotten way ahead of themselves on this one. "Well I don't want to take up your whole morning. But next time you're out that way, give that western beach an extra look."

"I'll do that," Applegate said enthusiastically. "And I'll pass it on to the guys on patrol out that way."

"Thanks," Hal said, and the two exchanged goodbyes.

A smear of sweat remained on the telephone receiver where Applegate had been holding it. And it lifted a film of dirt from the plastic that begged to be wiped away. But Applegate was too busy concentrating to attend to such details. He was digesting the phone call like a snake that had just swallowed a big meal. *I was calm, wasn't I? And straightforward. Noble knew I was out there recently. And maybe that's all he knows. Shit. What if he knows more? God, I could've just spilled on those two Miami assholes and been done with this whole thing. If those guys didn't have proof that I was out there. . . . just gotta stay calm and think through this. That's all."*

Applegate spent the next thirty minutes considering his options. He even jotted down some quick notes which he crumpled up and tossed into the trash. He had made his decision. It was time to call Winslow Greene in Miami.

Hal was relieved to have the phone call behind him, but he was still no closer to solving the Pavilion Key turtle nest mystery. While Applegate didn't deny having a familiarity with Pavilion Key, he didn't fulfill Hal's fantasy and confess to some crazy sea turtle egg scheme either. This one was going to take some more work. And most likely a surprise visit to the Applegate residence.

EIGHTEEN

WINSLOW GREENE DROPPED HIS OBESE FORM INTO THE worn naugahyde chair with a thud. "Greene here," he mumbled into the phone as a fleshy hand wiped a thick wad of sweat from his forehead. He had spent the last hour in the jungle-like heat and humidity of the main animal room at Dade Reptiles and Exotics. The ringing phone, broadcast via a loudspeaker system, had come as welcome relief since it afforded him a chance to cool down in his air-conditioned office. After a lengthy pause, Greene added, "You wanna do *what*?"

"They're on to me here, Winslow," Dean Applegate said in a desperate voice. "I gotta get rid of this shit. I'm bringing the eggs to *you*."

"Well. . . . I never hatched no sea turtles. What if I screw 'em up?"

"They're only days from hatching," Applegate said with authority. "You can't mess things up at this point. Just wait 'til they hatch and sell 'em."

Greene thought about this for a minute. "Okay. I'll do it. But I'm gonna take a bigger cut if I gotta do all that.

'Stead of sixty percent. I want seventy-five percent of every hatchling I sell. Seventy-five hundred per."

Applegate was prepared for something like this and reluctantly agreed to Greene's terms. At this point he'd be happy to get out of this whole crazy project with twenty or thirty thousand dollars, a bum leg, and his life. His big problem was the crazy guy on the island. He couldn't afford having those two criminals running around with the pictures they had of him on Pavilion Key, so he'd just have to go back out to the island and tell them about the change in plans. He'd still give them their two thirds cut. And if they didn't like it, they could take it up with Winslow Greene directly. That's the best he could do. Of course, he did neglect to tell *Greene* about the Pavilion Key thugs.

Applegate decided the sooner he could get rid of the eggs, the better. Using the leg injury as an excuse, he planned to take a half day off from work to "see a doctor" the following day. He knew that he could drive to Greene's place and back in time to be at work by one o'clock.

Hal knew his next step in the investigation had to be an unannounced visit to the Applegate's place. A little bold, but necessary. If Applegate had something to hide it would be obvious. If he was open and forthcoming—honest— Hal would know that he wasn't their guy. He decided to head over to see Applegate on a Tuesday night about eight o'clock. After dinner but still light out.

It was a typical south Florida August evening when Hal pulled into the Applegate's driveway. The air seemed paralyzed by the moisture that hung in it. The wild sounds of cicadas and frogs, both native and exotic, penetrated the stillness every few seconds. Hal surveyed the well landscaped property and focused on the children's toys which were scattered about like a contemporary art exhibit. Then he walked slowly from the crush and run gravel driveway to a neat brick walkway leading to the front door. He delivered a quick but firm report with the tail of a fish-shaped brass door knocker.

Over the vocalizations of a small dog, Hal heard a woman's voice shouting, "Coming! Hold on a second."

The door opened wide and Susan Applegate was standing there on one long slender leg while she used the other to shepherd a yapping Jack Russell terrier away from the portal to the outside world.

"Hi! Hal Noble from Game and Fish," Hal said in a friendly tone, keeping one eye on the frustrated Jack Russell as he extended his right hand towards Mrs. Applegate.

"Susan Applegate," she said, taking Hal's hand and delivering a firm shake. "I assume you're here to see Dean?"

"That's right. I'm working on a case I thought he might be able to help me with. We've met a couple of times over the years."

"Please come in. And don't mind the mess. Or this pain-in-the-butt dog. He's always like this around strangers," she said as she finally gave up trying to subdue the persistent hound, which by then was jumping at Hal's kneecaps like some sort of trained circus creature. "His name is 'Permit.' After the game fish."

Hal followed Susan into the kitchen. "Right. Interesting name. Sure is the friendly sort."

Susan faced Hal and gestured towards the kitchen table. "Have a seat. Dean should be back any minute. He just went to the store for some bottled water. We don't drink the stuff out of the well. One of the reasons we're moving to Marco. Better water." Susan moved towards the double-doored refrigerator and grabbed a long vertical handle. "Can I get you something to drink?"

"Oh, no. I'm good. Just had dinner," Hal said politely. "So you're buying a place on Marco?"

"Yes. Finally," Susan said with a sigh of relief. She liked the young Game and Fish Officer immediately and was glad to be chatting with him. Even flirting a bit. "We've been talking about it for years. And now we've got enough saved up to buy a nice place on one of the canals. Swimming pool too. Of course, we'll have to sell this house first."

"I bet Marco's a great place to live," Hal said trying to conceal his real feelings for the trendy development that obliterated the natural beauty of the largest island among the Ten Thousand Islands. "Nice place to raise a family," he continued. "And city water, too."

"Yes. The children are looking forward to the move," Susan said, taking a seat at the kitchen table across from Hal. "Except they're afraid they'll miss their neighborhood friends. Which they will for a while I'm sure. They're out playing with their friends as we speak."

"And their names?"

"Dean Jr. and Jennifer. Twelve and ten. Jennifer's the older one."

"You know the home you have isn't too shabby," Hal said, turning the conversation. "What is it, four bedrooms?"

"Yup. Four bedrooms. Two and a half baths, and a double garage. But Dean converted the garage into a reptile room a few years back."

Hal shifted in his chair and leaned slightly forward. "Reptile room? That sounds interesting. Mind if I see it?"

Susan began wringing her fingers. "Well. Yes. I

mean . . . yes I mind. Well, I mean, no *I* don't mind. But Dean would. Might. Look. He calls the place his garden and nobody's allowed in there if he's not with them. Even the kids and me. I know it sounds a little odd, but that's the rule."

Hal leaned back in his chair. "I see."

"Dean says there's lots that can go wrong with a reptile room," Susan continued, making an effort to defend her husband, even though she thought the whole reptile room situation was ridiculous for a grown man. "An animal could escape. Or someone could bring a disease into the room if they weren't careful. But I'm sure he'll show you around when he gets here."

But Dean Applegate never arrived to see Hal that night. Shortly after Hal arrived, Dean drove towards his house but made a quick U-turn when he spotted the Game and Freshwater Fish vehicle parked in his driveway. Then he sped out of the East Naples development and headed south towards the Tamiami Trail.

Noble was on to him. He was sure of it.

Applegate flattened the accelerator, launching the Fish and Wildlife Service Ford Explorer from a full stop at the blinking light on the Tamiami Trail to nearly seventy miles an hour on the asphalt ribbon that was Route 29. The two lane highway neatly bisected the Big Cypress Preserve and was the only link between the Trail and Alligator Alley, twenty miles to the north.

He was certain Susan knew nothing of the baby sea turtle project but he was equally certain that Hal Noble was closing in. The veteran Game and Fish officer's "woods sense" was common knowledge among local law enforcement. But all the "woods sense" in the state wasn't going to help Noble with *this* case. The evidence was gone! Tucked away in some corner of Winslow Greene's stuffy warehouse. Yet, he still had a nagging sense of worry about what might happen later on. Especially if someone like Noble traced the cash that would be coming his way after Greene sold the hatchlings.

After several minutes of concentrated thought, a smile creased Applegate's face when the idea occurred to him simply to cut his losses and dump the whole project. Greene would be tickled to keep whatever he could get for the turtles. And the two idiots on Pavilion Key would be content with their cut from Greene—which would no doubt be bigger if *he* weren't in the equation. A return to the less risky avocation of bribe collecting and looking the other way seemed pretty good to Applegate right now. Hell. The ridleys would keep coming back to Pavilion Key. And if things cooled down in the future—who knew—he just might sell a few baby sea turtles some day.

Dean had the whole thing figured, and for the first time in weeks, he was somewhat content. Like learning that a late summer hurricane had turned back to sea at the last moment, an ominous burden had been lifted from his shoulders. He decided to have a celebratory cigarette, so he reached for the pack he had stashed in the glove compartment. Distracted, he barely saw the radio-collared Florida panther dart in front of the Explorer. Instinctively, he jerked the wheel, just enough to avoid the big cat, but too much to maintain control of the three ton vehicle which swerved from side to side like a running drunkard before tumbling into the swollen canal on the right side of the road.

The impact of the air bag and horn plate shattered Applegate's right arm above the elbow and he was unable to disengage his seat belt. After several minutes, the inverted Explorer sank to the bottom of the canal, submerged and out of sight. Dean struggled furiously, trapped upside down in his seat, while the warm green water lapped at his hair and forehead. Soon his face was engulfed by the fatal liquid and he held his breath in a final desperate attempt to sustain himself. The metabolic processes in his body continued to produce carbon dioxide, the stimulus for breathing in mammals, while they used up the dwindling oxygen supply in his bloodstream. Still conscious after nearly two minutes with his nose and mouth submerged, Applegate's involuntary need to blow off carbon dioxide and obtain oxygen overwhelmed his will to keep the water out. A frantic fatal gasp pulled a deadly liter of canal water along his trachea and into his lungs, flooding the thousands of microscopic alveoli where gas exchange occurs. Seconds later, Applegate was unconscious, and like the camp light mantle deprived of propane, the glow in his brain faded slowly over the next several minutes until the last oxygen-starved neuron expired.

Dean Applegate had drowned.

NINETEEN

DEAN APPLEGATE HAD BEEN MISSING FOR THREE DAYS. Vanishing from his world like dew on a sultry Florida morning.

Hal spent about an hour exchanging small talk with Susan Applegate several nights earlier—finally taking leave of the worried wife with an uncomfortable promise to call her the next day to see how Dean was. And to schedule another visit (even though the element of surprise had evaporated and when Dean returned, he would surely clean up the reptile room—assuming there was anything "dirty" to clean up).

After twenty-four hours, Susan reported Dean missing, and a search for him and the Explorer were begun immediately. Since Applegate was a federal law enforcement officer, the effort to locate him was unusually thorough and far reaching. Of course the early stages of the investigation centered on the Applegate's home and a complete inspection of the reptile room turned up nothing unusual or remarkable.

Hal was given access to the police reports since a

friend of his was a big shot detective with the Collier County Sheriff's Office. The whole situation seemed very strange—even to Hal who had reason to suspect Applegate of some questionable activity.

Neil Hess almost dropped his bag of groceries at the check-out counter of the Everglades City Market when a casual glance of the Naples Daily News revealed a front page story about a missing U.S. Fish and Wildlife Officer named Dean Applegate. Cursing under his breath, Hess fumbled in his pocket for some change and snatched one of the papers from a pile on the floor, tossing two quarters onto the counter in the direction of the startled cashier. Then he hustled out the front door, placed the groceries on the ground, and began to read about Applegate.

"Slippery bastard," he muttered aloud. "Didn't think he was stupid enough to try something like this."

As Hess read on, he wasn't surprised to learn that there were no leads in the case—and that a meticulous search of the officer's home turned up nothing. Hess was certain that Applegate had split with the hatchlings, sold 'em, and was off in hiding some place. But he couldn't resolve Applegate's thinking. The photographic evidence he and Baker had would finish Applegate's career—and likely land him behind bars for at least a couple of years. The only thing Hess could come up with as he powered the Zodiac back to Pavilion Key was the remote possibility that Applegate would return, looking for Baker and him. "Nah," he said shaking his head. *This guy was weak. A coward. No way he'd have the balls to try something like that.*

Still, Hess was relieved to see a typically healthy and moronic Bobby Baker waiting on the beach to help stow the Zodiac and unload the supplies.

148

Another interesting and seemingly unrelated event took place the day after Applegate disappeared. A group of Outward Bound canoeists paddling about the Ten Thousand Islands discovered an algae covered light blue kayak nestled among a clump of mangroves about two miles north and west of Pavilion Key.

A harmless barrage of tiny waves, progeny from the small aluminum armada, lapped at the wayward kayak which had settled in a thick stew of intertidal muck, mangrove leaves, and oyster shells. After some friendly debate among the high school-aged adventurers and their twenty-three year old leader, the decision was made to tow the kayak back to the Outward Bound facility on the Barron River in Everglades City and call the authorities.

"Can't we at least make a search of it, Paula?" whined one persistent teenager. "Maybe we'll find some identification? Figure out who the owner is."

Paula Hayward, the attractive and unusually fit leader of the group, finally relented. "Oh. I guess it wouldn't hurt anything. But just one of you. And I'll supervise."

They didn't find much of interest on the initial search. Some maps and general camping supplies; rope, a single burner cook stove, canned goods, a few gallons of freshwater, eating utensils, a waterproof flashlight. Then the camper conducting the kayak exploration located a small, well concealed compartment near the port gunwale. Two exposed rolls of film lay neatly in tandem at the bottom of the small nook. Adding to the mystery of this lost kayak were the brownish red smudgy fingerprints which covered the thirty-five millimeter Kodak cassettes.

"Let's develop the film!" shouted one eager young Sherlock Holmes. "Maybe there's some pictures of the kayak's owner?"

Another excited teenager chimed in, "Yeah! And then we could find him and get a big reward!"

Paula Hayward had graduated from Bowdoin College in Maine the year before with a degree in history. Although still quite young, she was a wise and savvy guide who had worked for Outward Bound during three of her college summers. She was used to working with energetic teenagers, and this group of twelve students was no different than the others. The girls all wanted to be *like* Paula and the boys all wanted to be *with* her. The perfect position to be in when trying to control a bunch of hormone-laden pubescent teens.

"Don't even *think* about disturbing that film you guys," Paula said, her blonde hair blowing gently across the smooth tanned skin of her rounded forehead. "We're leaving everything the way we found it. Now secure the kayak to one of the canoes and let's head home."

After the string of seven canoes returned to the Outward Bound campus late that afternoon, Paula and one of the boys towed the kayak to the Outward Bound dock in Everglades City. There was a phone at the dock which was linked directly to the Outward Bound facility a quarter mile away on the opposite side of the Barron River. This was the way arriving campers and visitors called the facility to be picked up by canoe or motorboat. A pair of parking spaces harbored the white Outward Bound ten-passenger vans.

Two Collier County sheriff's deputies were waiting for Paula at the dock, and after asking her a few questions and taking some notes, they loaded the kayak into the back of their pickup and headed for the Everglades City sheriff's sub-station.

While in town, Paula decided to make a couple of

150

phone calls, including one to a friend and college class-mate who was a summer journalist intern with the Naples Daily News. Paula owed her a call, and during their conversation, she mentioned the kayak encounter since it was the most memorable thing that happened that day. The aspiring reporter smelled a story—especially the part about the exposed rolls of film with the suspicious fingerprints—and she peppered Paula with detailed questions including the names of the sheriff's deputies. Paula tried to play down the incident, since she thought of it as no more than a stray kayak in the Ten Thousand Islands, but she provided what information she could before hanging up and heading back to the isolated Outward Bound site.

Bobby Baker hadn't seen a newspaper in over two weeks, so he happily plodded through every column of the paper which Neil Hess had discarded after finishing with the Applegate article. On the last page of the Metro Section, there was a small piece with the headline: **Abandoned kayak turns up in Everglades National Park.**

"Hey boss! You might wanna take a look at this," Baker said, waving the folded newspaper in Hess's direction.

Hess didn't even look up from his torn folding lawn chair. "I don't need to see no more of that damn paper. If you'd leave me be, maybe I could figure out what we're gonna do about that idiot Ranger Rick."

Baker hesitated, then walked slowly to the seated Hess and stuck the newspaper in front of him with a grubby finger pointed to the small, boldface headline. "It's about that kayak we never found."

Hess stared at the newspaper for a moment without looking at Baker, then he snatched the paper away from him and quickly read the two paragraph article. "Shit.

They found some damn film! Jesus Christ. What the hell *else* can go wrong?"

Baker was silent, but knew the part about the exposed rolls of film would really piss Hess off.

"We've gotta go find that body and get it out to deeper water. Or maybe bury it here on the island," Hess said with pain in his voice. "There's no way to know what's on that film. But pictures of the dead guy and pictures of us digging on the beach could really make things messy. 'Specially if they find a body. And there's no doubt they'll start looking for one when that guy turns up missing." Then a flicker of a smile parted Hess's crusty lips. "But. No body. No murder rap. Just some circumstantial evidence—which we could beat if we do things smart. I sure hope you still got those GPS numbers written down somewhere."

Baker shifted his weight and stuffed his hands in his pockets. "I got 'em, boss."

Lydia and Hal hadn't seen each other for over two weeks, and for the first time in her life, Lydia Phillon found herself placing a man ahead of her career. She was supposed to be up in Melbourne doing more loggerhead nest survey work, but found herself canceling at the last minute, assigning the work to one of her grad students.

A surprise visit. How romantic she thought as she wondered what had happened to the *old* Lydia. The woman of science. Independent. Immune to vulnerability. Now acting like a love-struck coed. But she couldn't help herself. Hal Noble had a grip on her like the jaws of a leatherback on a moon jelly.

Hal picked up the beeping phone receiver from its plastic cradle. Ten of five on a Friday afternoon. It almost never failed. The week's paperwork was finished, and he

152

was looking forward to a gym workout and then a quiet evening at home; however, there was always some last minute Friday emergency that spoiled his plans. Reports of a poacher. Someone lost in the woods. A superior that needed to see him. So the sound of Lydia's soft voice on the other end of the line was like a gift. A bonus. A great way to end a hectic week.

"Busy day?" she said sympathetically.

Hal smiled into the receiver. "Usual stuff. The Pavilion Key situation still has me stumped. How about you? On your way to Melbourne?" Hal could tell by the connection that she was on her mobile phone.

"Well. I'm on the road. But not to Melbourne. Got any dinner plans?"

Puzzled, Hal replied, "Dinner? Plans? Probably just some leftovers and ice cream. Why? You gonna order me a pizza?"

Lydia was excited and could barely harness her enthusiasm. "Look. It's nearly five. Why don't you wrap things up and walk out to your truck? I've arranged for a surprise."

Hal figured he would play along. "Okay. Sounds interesting. I'll shut things down and head right for the parking lot. Should I call you after I see my surprise?"

At that moment Lydia was pulling off of the Tamiami Trail and into the ranger station entrance. "Sure. I really want to see what you think of it."

When Hal opened the front door and saw Lydia sitting on the hood of her car, her smooth legs swinging back and forth with her hands placed innocently under her thighs, his heart felt like it had been perfused with tepid water and the warmth radiated throughout his body.

"So what kind of pizza did you have in mind?" Lydia

said, thrilled with her big surprise and smiling broadly at the effect she was having on Hal. "'Cause I was thinking about a nice romantic dinner at the Port O' the Islands Cheekee Hut."

"What a. . . . I can't believe it!" Hal shouted as he jumped from the front step of the Ranger station and jogged toward Lydia. "This is great! Of course we can go to the Cheekee Hut. Or any place else."

Having not seen each other in a while, the new lovers fondled each other's hands during dinner like a pair of sparring beetles. Lydia shared her most recent academic triumphs and frustrations while Hal volleyed back tidbits of the Pavilion Key situation and the strange disappearance of Dean Applegate.

"So no trace of him, huh?" Lydia said.

"Nothing. No phone calls. No sign of his vehicle. Just vanished," Hal said shrugging his shoulders. "It's like a big bird came by, scooped him up—Explorer and all—and dropped him a thousand miles from here."

Lydia put down her fork and dabbed her lips with a paper napkin. "You *still* think he's involved in the ridley nest mystery?"

"More so than ever. Just can't put it all together. I've had Jasper run by the Pavilion Key beach every couple days for the past week or so. Hasn't seen a thing out of the ordinary."

Lydia picked up her fork again and stabbed at a thick piece of flaky grouper. "Listen Hal. I'd like to head out there this weekend. The Rancho Nuevo ridleys are due to hatch out in a couple of weeks. So I'm thinking these ridleys should go about the same time. If I'm going to document this and get it published, I'll need photos and video of the hatchlings crawling across the sand and . . ."

Hal politely cut Lydia off. "Excuse me, but, do you think that's a good idea? Getting the word out so fast? I mean. Pavilion Key's a small island. In no time it'd be crawling with herpetologists, wildlife photographers, you name it."

Lydia went on the defensive. "Hey. Didn't you use the 'p' word to get me down here in the first place? 'A unique publishable opportunity,' I recall hearing you tell me on the phone."

Hal couldn't conceal a slight grin. "You're right. I did say that. And, well, you *should* publish it. But don't rush into anything. That's all I ask."

"All right," Lydia said smiling. "I understand you want to protect Pavilion Key. And I do too. But I still need to at least collect the data while it's available. I already have pictures of the poached nest and the egg shells, as well as the dead embryos you saved for me. And I'll need to get shots of the females coming to nest next spring in order to complete the report. How about if I agree not to write up anything until we at least know how many nesting females there are?"

"Okay. You've got a deal," a relieved Hal said. He knew how important this information could be to Lydia's career. He just wanted her to spend some time thinking about the ramifications of making the information public. A little time might allow them to figure out the best way to protect the nests in the future. And discover who was doing the poaching and why. "I'll take you out to Pavilion Key tomorrow or Sunday. You pick."

"How about Sunday," Lydia said, raising her mug of Swamp Ale in the air. "I was thinking about sleeping in tomorrow."

TWENTY

WHAT THE HELL DO YOU MEAN YOU CAN'T TELL IF IT'S A four or a nine you idiot!" Neil Hess yelled at the cringing Bobby Baker. "You better guess right. 'Cause we gotta find that body. And I don't wanna be out here forever looking for it."

Baker knew he had to come up with an answer. "Pretty sure it's a nine," he said. But of course he had no idea. The GPS coordinates he had scribbled down when they sunk Mantis's body were 25° 42′ 09″ latitude and 81° 20′ 55″ longitude. He had left the nine "open." So it could just as easily have been a four since that's how he made them. The error translated into little more than two hundred yards. Not a big distance in general maritime navigation. But a huge problem for two guys up to their armpits in sea water, pushing a Zodiac, and feeling the bottom for a submerged body with their shuffling, muck-laden feet.

They had been wading back and forth for over an hour trying to find Mantis in water as dark as lentil soup. And nearly as hot. All they had to show for their effort were a couple of oyster shell-stubbed toes and a few globs of seaweed. Neil Hess was as pissed off as Baker had ever seen him.

"Look. This ain't working for shit. So here's what we're gonna do," Hess snapped. We're gonna make believe that number of yours is a four! And we're gonna go check out *that* spot. But this time, you're gonna stay in the boat and keep us on track. Think you can do that?"

"Yeah."

"Good. I'll stay in this piss water. And we're gonna do what's called an expanding square search around the GPS spot. Every time I take ten steps, you're gonna turn the boat ninety degrees. When we get back to the beginning we change to fifteen steps. Then twenty. Got it?"

"Yeah. I think so," was Baker's timid reply. He actually had the basic idea and hoped he could figure out the details as the process unfolded. Or even better, they'd find the body right away and he'd be off the hook.

Hess walked slowly behind the Zodiac, holding the transom with his hands, the lower unit of the shut-off outboard gently parting the water in front of him. They were on the third leg of the ten step part of the pattern when Neil Hess let out a scream that could have busted half the crystal in the ritzy Naples Saks Fifth Avenue store, forty miles away.

Baker, who was keeping the bow straight with a paddle and listening to Hess count off steps, lurched around midway through Hess's high decibel screeching moan of agony. Baker had no way of knowing it, but Hess had just been seriously wounded by a large southern stingray.

The southern stingray, *Dasyatis americana,* will reach a length of ten feet and can deliver an unbelievably excruciating wound with either or both of its serrated, venomous spines, located near the base of its whip-like tail. The

stingray that Neil Hess had the unfortunate luck of kicking
in the head was over eight feet wide at the wing tips and
weighed nearly seventy pounds. Stingrays are not aggressive creatures by nature, but when disturbed, they will flex
their tail like a piece of bent willow and use the recoil to
ram a long tail spine into the tissues of their perceived at-
tacker. Stingray spines have been found securely embed-
ded in shark jaws, sea turtle shells, and dolphin skulls. The
larger spine on Neil Hess's sting ray was over six inches
long and covered with a thin layer of toxic epithelium and
proteinaceous goo.

Hess was perfectly situated for a horrible sting. His
right leg was well planted in the Gulf bottom ooze when his
left foot accidentally kicked the meaty cartilaginous fish as
it was moving slowly towards him hunting for a crustacean
lunch. The ray instinctively flexed its tail rapidly to the
right and then hurled it lightning quick to the left, burying
the large spine deep into Neil Hess's ankle. In fact, the
strike was delivered with such force that the bony spine
penetrated Hess's tibia right to the marrow before snap-
ping off. About an inch of the spine was left sticking out of
the bleeding hole in Hess's lower leg.

According to people who have been wounded by sting
rays, there is no animal-inflicted experience which is more
painful. And this includes venomous snake bites, jellyfish
stings, and even maulings by large carnivores. There is a
true account of a South American native who was stung in
an Amazon river tributary by a relatively small freshwater
sting ray. The pain and discomfort were so great that the
poor fellow tried to kill himself by repeatedly running
head first into a nearby tree. He wasn't successful, but did
manage to knock himself out, providing some temporary

relief from the agony. This story also helps to explain Neil Hess's next response.

"Kill me! Kill me goddammit!" Hess yelled in between the incredible moans and screams. Tears were streaming down the sides of his pale white face and he twirled slowly from side to side like a broken carnival ride. "Oh. God! You gotta kill me, Baker. I can't take this pain. Ahhhhhhhhhh!"

Bobby Baker was in a state of disbelief. What the hell had happened? Hess was going crazy! If he didn't do what Hess said, he'd be in really big trouble. He calmly placed the paddle across the bow of the Zodiac, walked over to the console area where Hess kept a loaded revolver, and retrieved the weapon from a plastic bag next to the driver's seat. Then he leaned over the transom, used both hands to aim the gun at Hess's head, and fired off a round at the twisting, screaming man.

Baker was not a particularly good shot, and shooting the .357 magnum double action didn't help matters much. But he did manage to hit Neil Hess square in the Adam's apple, which had the immediate effect of turning the loud screaming into a more tolerable muffled gurgling. With Hess staring at Baker with wide eyes popping out of a now even paler face, Baker fired a second round, which ripped through Hess's head just below his nose. This time the force of the projectile knocked Hess backwards, off his good foot, and onto his back. A small geyser of blood, mucus, and saliva spurted from the neck wound for several seconds before dissipating to nothing more than a trickle. Neil Hess was dead.

Baker just stared at the floating corpse for several minutes, which appeared to be getting smaller, since the Zodiac was drifting much faster than the waterlogged body. It wasn't until Hess started to sink that Baker grabbed the paddle and made his way back to the dead man, just in time to hook his clothing with a small gaff that was kept aboard. Pulling Hess's body against one of the pontoons, Baker was able to secure it to a floating seat cushion using some nearby cord. Then he let Hess slip back into the murky water, untethered, and floating harmlessly a few feet from the Zodiac.

Now what was he gonna do?

Bobby Baker almost never made a decision for himself. His divorced mother recognized that he wasn't the brightest kid from an early age, so she sheltered him, while his more intelligent siblings were free to test the world around them. He didn't have many friends. None, really. And his younger sister was allergic to dogs, cats, and apparently anything else with hair. So traditional pets were out too. His only companion from the time he was six years old through his early teens was a red-eared slider which his mother had purchased for him at a Woolworth's department store. He treasured his turtle friend, and cared for it meticulously, until the allergic sister borrowed it for show and tell one day. The classroom trouble-maker dropped it out of a third story window to see if the turtle would break open. It did.

In high school, before he dropped out at the age of sixteen, Baker hung out with a group of kids lead by a punk of a character who got the small gang involved with drugs and petty crimes. Bobby did whatever the alpha male said, which landed him in jail on two occasions. And Baker, like a bicycle tire stuck in an edged sidewalk, just couldn't find his way out of the crime rut.

He actually met Neil Hess in a Florida prison, and the two hooked up about a year later when they were both on the outside. But now there was no one to turn to for direction. No over-protective mom. No teacher staying late for detention duty. No pot-smoking teenage messiah. No empathetic prison guard. Baker was like a lone sheep, miles from his flock. And the shepherd was dead. Half-floating a few feet away, a small halo of blood-stained water surrounding his traumatized head.

As mentally sluggish as Bobby Baker was, he did recognize the fact that he had just killed a man. And that he could get in a shit load of trouble for it. *He* was a murderer. Up until now, Hess had done all the killing. So Baker never really thought much about the consequences of killing someone. Or what to do with the body for that matter. Now he had both issues straining the weak, loosely woven fibers of his brain. Christ! He didn't even know what had made Hess beg for a mercy killing. But it must have been pretty bad.

Baker never completely grasped the whole search pattern concept. But he was intelligent enough to know that floating around in the Gulf of Mexico with a dead man tied to your boat wasn't the best way to stay out of jail. So after mulling things over like a child trying to decide on which box of cereal to pick for the shopping cart, he eventually elected to abandon the search for Mantis and tow Hess's body out to deeper water. Where he would sink him. The only problem with the plan was that he hadn't factored in the school of brown sharks that Hess's sanguine soup had attracted.

Baker dragged Hess about a mile out to sea, still well within sight of land and only a paddle poke to the bottom, when the first hungry elasmobranch took a chunk out of Neil Hess. Baker didn't see the attack, but like a fisherman trolling for bass with a surface plug, he felt it. By the time he idled down the Zodiac and turned back to take a look, a school of six, man-sized sharks were taking turns whittling Neil Hess away like a block of human suet. Now things had really become complicated. And Baker was worried the sharks might take after him at any moment. So he simply cut the line that connected him to the gruesome floating buffet, turned the Zodiac around, and headed back to the relative safety and stability of Pavilion Key.

During the short ride back to the island, he kept remembering Neil Hess's saying, "No body. No murder." And it made him feel a little better about everything.

About the same time the brown sharks were devouring Neil Hess, the reverse was happening in the darkroom of the Collier County Sheriff's Office in Naples, where a two dimensional Hess, alive and intact, had just appeared, waving a hand over a larger man stuffing a shovel into the sand.

Sergeant Wayne Harper, the lab specialist for the department, had separated the shots with the people in them from the close-ups of osprey and alligators. He walked into an adjacent office, tossed a half dozen four by six glossy prints onto the desk where another officer was pecking away at a computer keyboard, and said, "Know these guys?"

"Nope. Never seen 'em," said Detective Chuck Wickler, who fingered through the small stack of pictures in about five seconds. "Looks like they're digging for buried treasure or something. This the stuff from that old beached canoe down in the Back Country?"

"Yeah. Actually, it was a sea kayak, detective. Found by some Outward Bound kids."

"Okay. Kayak. Canoe. Whatever," Wickler said, pushing back from his desk. "This all there is?"

"All the rest were nature shots. Birds and stuff like that."

"What about this tall, skinny guy," Wickler said, picking up the prints and singling out a photograph of Mantis standing next to a sign reading, 'Flamingo, Eastern Gateway to the Everglades.' "He's not in the other pictures."

Harper leaned over the detective's left shoulder. "Yeah. I was wondering about this one," he said, pointing a finger at the bottom corner of the print. "Plus. Look at the date. It was taken almost two weeks before the others."

"Flamingo. That's the place down south of Florida City. Right?" Wickler said, looking up at Harper.

"Yeah. About a hundred mile boat ride from Everglades City."

"But, it's still in the National Park, isn't it?"

"Yup. Sure is. Some great boardwalks too. Ever been there?"

"Not much into the wild outdoors, Harper. My idea of a nature hike is six thousand yards around a nice golf course. And the more trees and woods I walk through, the less fun I'm havin'. Know what I mean?"

"Yes, sir."

"Now. Know anybody who works for the Park Service?"

Harper scratched at his cheek. "Not exactly. But I used to play softball with a guy named Randy Wells who works for Marine Fisheries down in the Everglades. Far as I know he spends most of his time in the Park. I could give him a call. See if he knows anybody in Flamingo. And I could make some dupes of these shots and get 'em passed around."

"Good. And see if you can blow these shots up a little. What d'ya call it when you do that?

"Cropping."

"Yeah right. Do some cropping so we can get a better look at the people," Wickler said, handing the small pile back to Harper. "And no need to mess with the plant and animal shots. We're in the business of finding humans."

"Yes, detective. I'm heading back to the darkroom right now. Should have these pics sprinkled around the Everglades by noon tomorrow."

"Good work, Harper."

Randy Wells wasn't in the habit of receiving FedEx packages. So he was somewhat surprised to find one lying on his desk at lunch time. Most of his Fisheries correspondence was handled by regular mail and fax. But this was no urgent letter from the home office in DC. The sender's address was listed as Detective Chuck Wickler, Collier County Sheriff's Office, Naples, FL.

Wells peeled open the package with a satisfying tug that sent micro particles of compressed paper into the surrounding air. Then he flexed open the heavy envelope to reveal a form cover letter and a half dozen four by six color snapshots. The letter was written on generic Sheriff's Office stationery and described the lost kayak, the found film, and the desire to identify the men in the pictures. There was also a short handwritten note on the photocopied letter from Wayne Harper, which read: "Randy, thanks for your help on this. If you recognize any of these guys, contact Det. Wickler at the above number. Still playing any ball? Regards, Wayne."

Randy smiled briefly, then began studying the photographs. As far as he knew these guys could have been anybody. He didn't recognize them at all. Fact was, he interviewed dozens of fishermen every day. They really all looked the same.

There wasn't much interesting about two guys digging in the sand. They could have been almost anywhere in the Ten Thousand Islands. And they sure didn't look like fishermen. But neither did the tall, skinny guy pictured in Flamingo. Yet something about him was. . . . unusual. Even captivating. He's by himself, Randy thought. Most folks who visited the Everglades had company. And he assumed that if the guy had a wife or some other companion, there'd be a picture of them in the packet too. Randy studied the man's face. He wasn't smiling, but he looked happy. At peace with the world around him.

Then something caught Randy's eye. A ring on the man's right hand. Bulky and shiny. With a palm frond-green stone stuck right in the middle of it. The same unusually colored gem that was seated in the catfish ring. "Jesus. Could it be?" Randy let the words slip through the small spaces between his teeth. He strained for more detail but there was none to be had. Even a handy magnifying glass only seemed to distort the image of the ring.

Without putting the photograph of Mantis down, Wells scanned the form letter and began dialing the number of Detective Chuck Wickler in Naples, thirty-five miles away.

"Wickler here," the gruff voice said on the other end of the line.

Randy was surprised to find that he was nervous. After all, what did he have to be nervous about? He'd talked to cocky gumshoes before. Once or twice anyway. "Randy Wells here. Down in Everglades City. I work for the National Marine Fisheries Service."

"So. You tryin' to find a missing fish or somethin'?" Wickler replied sarcastically, thinking someone had forwarded this guy to the wrong office. "This is the Collier County Sheriff's Detective branch. And *I'm* a detective."

"I know," Wells said calmly. "I'm calling to talk to *you,* Detective Wickler. Your name and number are on this letter that just got FedExed to me. Along with some photographs."

"Right! Wells! Harper's buddy," Wickler replied, sitting up in his chair and trying to apologize for his sarcastic tone without actually saying he was sorry. "That Harper's right on top of things. We were talking about you only yesterday. Got anything for me on those pictures?"

Wells took a deep breath. "Okay. This is gonna sound really weird. But one of the guys is wearing a big, unusual looking ring."

"So what's weird about that? A lot of guys are wearing jewelry these days. Surprised it's not through his nose. But then I would've noticed *that.*"

"Right. The weird thing is that about a week ago, some guy is gutting a catfish at the dock in Chokoloskee, and this gold ring with a big green stone pops outta the fish's stomach."

"Yeah? It's gettin' weirder."

"Well. The ring on the hand of the lanky guy looks a lot like the ring that the lucky fisherman found."

"Hmmmm. Do you have the fisherman's name?"

"That's the neat part. I do!" Wells semi-shouted into the phone. "We write down everything about these guys except their underwear size. And I'm sure next year some paper pusher in Washington will add that to the list. Anyway, I made a note about the catfish ring, being so unusual and all. So it shouldn't take me long to track down the guy's

166

info. Just a matter of flipping through last week's data sheets."

"How long's not too long?"

"Should have it for you within the hour," Wells said confidently. "And there's something else you'll probably like.

"Oh? What's that?"

"The ring was likely some kind of company performance reward. So many years of service kinda thing. Don't remember the details. And there may have been some initials or something carved on the inside too."

"That could certainly come in handy," Wickler said, his interest in the case rising to the next level. "When you find that data sheet, would you mind faxing it to me? I wouldn't want to miss anything—plus I'm curious about how much shit they make you guys ask these poor bastards."

Wells snickered at Wickler's dry humor. "Soon as I dig it up I'll fax it right over. Then I'll call you in case you've got any questions. I think you'll be able to find the catfish connoisseur with no trouble at all."

TWENTY-ONE

Y EAH. THAT'S ME," MIKE BARBER SAID, ANSWERING THE simple question posed by the man on the other end of the line, who identified himself as Detective Wickler. "How can I help ya?"

Barber was a forty-three year old plumber with a beer gut and a kind heart who owned a modest home on the outskirts of Fort Lauderdale. A simple family man with a wife and two elementary school-aged kids, Barber lived for three things: time with his children, football season, and fishing with his buddies. And he had a lot of buddies. So it was understandable that he wanted to get as much mileage as possible out of the catfish ring. Talking about it. Showing it off. Even letting his pals photograph him with it on.

"I'm holding a National Marine Fisheries Service survey sheet that says you found a ring in the belly of a catfish down in Chokoloskee last week," Chuck Wickler said, getting right to the point.

Barber hesitated. He had intended to track down the ring's rightful owner. Really. Heck, he'd only had it now a little over a week, and he just planned to keep it the rest of the summer—after all, it was his favorite on-the-job story. "Uhhh. That's right. But I ain't done nothin' illegal. The ring was in my fish and. . . ."

Wickler cut him off. "Mr. Barber. Did I say you broke the law in any way?"

"Well. No. But . . ."

"That ring. Your ring. Might be helpful in a missing person's investigation. Randy Wells, the Fisheries guy who took your information, says he remembers that some words were engraved on the ring. We just wanna know what those words are. You still got it?"

"Oh sure. Yeah. Makes a pretty good story and all. . . ."

"I'm sure it does. Now can you get the ring and tell me what it says?"

"Okay. I have it in my truck. Can ya hang on a minute?"

"I'll be right here," Wickler said, tapping his pencil on the desk top and swiveling from side to side in his chair.

Barber got the ring and read the raised inscription surrounding the cut periodot stone, as well as the date and initials scratched on the inside of the ring. "Ya know, I was gonna try and find the owner. Just haven't—"

"Don't worry about it Mr. Barber. We'll call you if we need you. Just don't lose the ring in the meantime. Okay?"

Barber sighed with relief. "No sir. I won't. I'll even keep it here in the house 'til you tell me what to do with it. All locked up."

Within an hour, Chuck Wickler had all the information he needed. The Komen Brewery in Milwaukee was a cinch to find, and one of the secretaries was able to confirm that the ring belonged to Hunter Ivan. Her description of Mantis matched the man photographed in Flamingo, and she confirmed that he had headed to Florida on a two week vacation—solo as far as she knew. He was now three days overdue for work. "Pretty unusual for a guy who was never even five minutes late," she said.

Wickler thanked the secretary for her assistance, hung up the phone, and let out a deep breath. *They had the guy's kayak, his film, and a ring. So where was he?*

When boats turned up empty in the Ten Thousand Islands, the owner was either in another boat, treading water, or dead. You just didn't leave your boat and stroll out of the Back Country on a dirt road or Boy Scout trail, like you might somewhere in New England or out West. Even a fit and well supplied person would have to be demented to set off through the nearly impenetrable mangrove forest in the middle of summer. Since Mantis hadn't turned up alive anywhere, chances were excellent that he was dead. Probably drowned.

Despite the futility of a body search in the organically rich Gulf of Mexico coastal waters, Chuck Wickler, like a school kid with a pile of homework, forced himself to initiate it. He'd even had to make arrangements to get the east coast plumber to show the searchers roughly where he caught the ring-bearing catfish.

In addition to the Collier County Sheriff's Office, Wickler enlisted the help of the marine patrol, Coast Guard, Civil Air Patrol, and the Florida Game and Fresh Water Fish Commission. Four boats in all. Dragging the bottom with hooks and nets. They agreed to spend two full days looking for a body. And that would be the end of it.

Hal Noble's contact at the Sheriff's Office had told him about the impending search. But Hal wasn't going to be involved. Another Game and Fish officer got the nod. Body searches in the Ten Thousand Islands were not uncommon events. But this one caught Hal's attention because of the proximity to Pavilion Key and the odd circumstances linking the catfish ring to the orphaned photograph. Otherwise, he was still focusing his efforts on the whereabouts of Dean Applegate and the mystery of the Pavilion Key ridley nests. He and Lydia had visited Pavilion Key that past Sunday, but the visit was uneventful. No nests had hatched out. And as far as they could tell, there had been no further poaching activity.

It was now Wednesday and Hal had decided to do a little patrol work on his way out to Pavilion Key. He also planned to drop in on the search team to check on their progress—even lend a hand if needed.

The sight of the persistent search vessels plying the waters off of Pavilion Key spooked Bobby Baker. *Someone must have seen me shoot Hess,* he thought. *And they'll surely be combing the island for me in no time.* He decided to make a break for the mainland.

Baker dragged the Zodiac from the campsite to the beach in what resembled a controlled panic. Physically, he was capable of most anything. But making the decisions was testing his limits. Still, he had enough sense to initially head south, away from the search party, then west and north toward Everglades City. Baker knew he could find the Indian Key Pass channel markers, eventually leading him to the Barron River. Chokoloskee Pass and Rabbit Key Pass, both tricky routes to the shell mound town of Chokoloskee, were much tougher to locate.

One didn't see many Zodiacs in the Ten Thousand

Islands—especially two miles off shore. Yet that was the image Hal's powerful binoculars captured and imprinted on the wildlife officer's retinas.

Hal had no trouble overtaking the plodding rubber craft and its lone occupant. "Turn off your engine please," Hal shouted, simultaneously drawing a finger across his neck and pointing to the outboard.

Baker killed the motor. *No body, no murder. No body, no murder.* The words jumped about in his head. His childhood instincts told him to leap into the surrounding water and escape. But his time with the criminally savvy Hess snuffed out the foolish impulse like a blanket on a pesky flame.

Hal maneuvered his twenty-two foot center console craft along the port side of the dinghy. He quickly scanned the small vessel, noting the lack of fishing gear and emergency flotation devices. The Zodiac did have a valid registration sticker, though.

"So where you headed?" Hal asked.

Never lie til ya have to, Hess always said. "Everglades City," was Baker's quick reply.

Almost everybody Hal pulled over—on the road and on the water—was nervous. Some more than others. But this guy had a strange calm about him. Like a seasoned school kid concealing a pack of cigarettes from an inquiring teacher.

"Okay. Can I see your registration card?"

Baker patted at his empty pockets for a moment. Then rummaged through a small compartment near the steering wheel. "Can't seem to find it. Must've left it at home."

"And where's home?"

"Uhhh. Miami."

"So where'd you put in? Not going to tell me you piloted this Zodiac here on six gallons of gas from Miami, are you?"

"No sir," Baker said slowly. "My car and trailer's in Everglades City."

"Well. Do you at least have a driver's license? Some kind of ID?"

"'Fraid I must've left my wallet in the car."

Hal's brow wrinkled. "With your life jacket?"

Baker looked about him. *Shit.* He and Hess used the flotation cushions for seats sometimes back at the campsite. "I could've sworn I put those cushions in the boat. Usually carry two. For safety ya know," Baker said with a sheepish grin.

"I'm afraid I'm going to have to write you up on these violations. But I can't do that 'til I know who you are. So get that engine going—I'll follow you in to Everglades. Are your vehicle and trailer at the public landing?"

"Uh. Yeah. The public landing," Baker said with resignation. "Ya sure ya gotta do that? I ain't botherin' nobody. Just out for a ride on the ocean."

"Everglades City. Let's go. You can do some more sightseeing on the way in."

Baker powered up the Zodiac and headed for Indian Key. Hal followed closely behind—at about ten knots—and radioed the ranger station with the details. In forty-five minutes they were idling up the Barron River towards the public boat ramp and parking area.

"Someone must've stole my car!" Baker shouted. He had no idea what else to say (the stolen pickup Hess and he used to bring the Zodiac to the Ten Thousand Islands had surely been returned to its owner weeks ago). With another Game and Fish officer standing by in a parked vehicle, he had no where to run, either.

Hal approached the officer sitting in the Blazer. "Call the Sheriff's Office. Got no choice but to turn this guy over to the County. We'll let them sort it out."

On Hal's orders, Baker remained in the Zodiac which was secured to the dock. A Sheriff's patrol car came along in five minutes and the deputy drove Baker to the Everglades City substation for questioning.

At the substation, Baker was placed in a locked room where he was asked to fill out some paperwork and told by the desk officer that a detective would be in to ask him some questions shortly. Then an interesting thing happened. The desk officer recognized Baker from the pictures that had been circulated from the Naples office. Just to be sure, he detached one of the photos from a nearby bulletin board and double checked it. Absolutely. The big guy in the picture was the same guy sitting in the questioning room. The desk officer had planned to have the local head deputy talk to the stranger, but the photo identification changed everything. He quickly reached for the phone and called Detective Wickler in Naples—who was grabbing for his hat and car keys even before he hung up the phone with the perceptive Everglades desk officer.

No body, no murder. No body, no murder. No body, no murder. Baker repeated the words in his mind like a mantra. He'd been locked in the room for over an hour. No one had come to question him. Not even a knock on the door. He was getting scared. The long delay in this rinky-dink town meant something was up.

Finally, nearly ninety minutes after being lead into the substation, the door opened and a large man in his mid-forties wearing dark sunglasses and medium sideburns stepped into the small room holding a manilla envelope. "I'm Detective Wickler. What's *your* story?"

"My name is Billy Becker. And I have no story. 'Cept for someone stealing my car with my wallet and everything." Since Baker had a criminal record in Florida, he didn't want to use his real name. Hess had picked out the alias months ago because it was easy for him to remember. The lie might buy him a little time. But just a little. His fingerprints would give him away eventually.

Wickler opened the envelope and tossed the set of prints onto the table in front of the seated Baker. "This guy sure looks like *you*," Wickler said, pointing to one of the photos with Baker and Hess digging in the sand. "Now, who's *this* guy?" Wickler had moved his index finger from Baker's image to Hess's.

Baker was silent.

"What about this fella?" Wickler said, corralling the picture of Mantis and placing it in front of Baker. "Ever see him before?"

Baker glanced at the picture, then at Wickler, eventually fixing his gaze on the white stucco wall behind the detective. He did not speak to Wickler again—never asked for a lawyer—not even a phone call. Nor did he hear the detective's persistent questions. The internal mantra had taken over his brain like a mischievous computer virus does a hard drive.

No body, no murder. No body, no murder. No body, no murder.

Detective Wickler had no choice but to arrest Baker and hold him for obstruction of justice. By the next day he learned the large silent man's true identity, and that he had spent a total of twenty months in Florida prisons, mostly for grand larceny. But he hadn't turned up on any wanted sheets for over two years. Baker's parole officer's report was satisfactory. Yet he wouldn't utter a single word. He ate and drank a little, but that was it. And the fixed gaze remained pretty much the same.

Two days of dragging the bottom where the catfish ring was found turned up a fishing rod and reel, thirteen lost crab traps, an old lawn chair, and several hundred feet of monofilament fishing line with attached sinkers, hooks, and swivels—but no corpse.

With the identification of two of the three men pictured in the kayak photos, and one very silent suspect in custody, Wickler decided to cut off the search for the missing brewery worker until they broke Baker down for more information.

TWENTY-TWO

Jasper Wiley left Everglades City once, maybe twice a year, usually to see his doctor in Naples for an annual physical. The owners of the Rod & Gun Club insisted on it—as long as he wanted to keep working, anyway. But he occasionally ventured into Everglades City to chat up old friends or buy a bottle of his favorite tequila at the local liquor store.

Word of the Baker arrest had spread like spilled beer over the small town—a little messy, but easy enough to clean. And it wouldn't leave much of a stain. Jasper heard the part about the photographs and decided to stop by the substation for a look. Curiosity mostly.

Duplicates of the original photographs had been laminated on a piece of red cardboard with a request from the Naples division of the Collier County Sheriff's Office to provide any information relating to the photos. *Blah, blah, blah, blah,* Jasper thought, too impatient to concentrate on the fine print. He was much more interested in the beach where the two men were apparently digging a hole. It was an island he knew well. Pavilion Key.

Jasper wanted to cooperate with the authorities, and help them out with the case, but after taking the time to read the details of the makeshift poster, he learned that the Sheriff's Office was specifically asking if anyone had seen or could identify the *men* in the photographs. So he didn't feel *too* bad about not providing them with the geographical information he had. He needed to speak with Hal first.

Although he couldn't be sure the unidentified men were digging over the ridley nesting area, it certainly seemed likely that these photos and the mysterious robbing of the sea turtle nests, were somehow related. *Hal would know how to handle it.*

At almost the same moment Jasper was examining Mantis's vacation pictures, Hal was stopping to pick up a hitchhiker on Route 29 about ten miles north of the Trail.

"Where ya headed?" Hal yelled through the open passenger window of the Blazer. Hitchhiking on Florida state roads wasn't illegal. Nor was picking hitchikers up—even for Florida Game and Fish officers—although it was frowned upon by the Commission.

The dark-skinned Latino man rested his sweaty elbows on the base of the vacant window frame. He was in his early twenties, had thick black hair which brushed the back and sides of his neck, and his jeans and white T-shirt were so clean they almost looked pressed. "Immokalee. Been workeen sugar cane up there for a couple months. Car broke down the other day and won't be ready for another week." Then the man presented Hal with a generous, gold tooth-capped smile.

Hal smiled back. "I can take you as far as the Alley.

Then I gotta turn around. Six, maybe seven miles. Will that help?"

"Oh, yes sir. Thank you," the grateful man replied as he opened the door and slid into the seat. He quickly secured his seat belt, then looked straight ahead.

Hal started up the Blazer and pulled back onto the simmering asphalt. "Good. What's your name?" Hal had hitched quite a lot when he was a college student at the University of Florida, frequently catching rides between school and his home in Jacksonville, so he empathized with these hopeful road walkers.

"Alfredo. Alfredo Luis Maria Gonzales. But my amigos call me Choo-Choo. You too, please."

"Alright. Choo-Choo it'll be."

Both men were silent for several minutes. Alfredo could plainly see Hal's name badge. "Officer Noble. I saw something back there, maybe a mile from where you picked me up, that I was going to report to police. But since you pick me up. Maybe I tell you?"

Hal kept his eyes on the road. "Okay, Choo-Choo. What was it?"

"Well. At first I thought it was just an old tire floating in the deetch. You know the water by the side of the road."

"Yeah, sure. The canal."

"Si. But when I look close I see two more tires. One ees out of the water about four eenches. The others maybe an eench or less." Alfredo was now holding the thumb and forefinger of his left hand about an inch apart. "So I think maybe ees an upside down car. What you think?"

Motor vehicles ended up in the roadside canals pretty frequently in southern Florida—so Alfredo's story was certainly worth following up. The area had also experienced a mini summer drought in that it hadn't rained in over a week. Most of the canals and other areas of standing water were down at least a foot.

"I'll be sure and check it out, Choo-Choo. Really appreciate the information."

"Oh. No probleem. I hope if ees a car, no one got hurt," Alfredo said, unbuckling his seat belt since they were slowing down to enter the exit for I-75, also known as the Alligator Alley. "And tanks again for the ride."

As soon as Alfredo stepped onto the sloping crushed coral shoulder and closed the door, Hal bid him goodbye and quickly made a U-turn, heading south to check out the hitchhiker's unusual report.

"She's lettin' go!" the beefy tow truck operator shouted to no one in particular. Just then the quarter inch braided steel cable came flying off of the large pulley attached to the top of the truck's lifting arm like a piece of spaghetti spinning off a fork. "Damn I hate these submerged son's of bitches. I'm gonna have to call in another truck."

Hal had located the submerged tires the hitchhiker talked about without difficulty and immediately contacted the Sheriff's Office and a towing company. From all indications, the tires did belong to an inverted and submerged vehicle. It had taken over an hour for the tow truck to arrive, and now they'd have to wait who knew how long for another truck to help hoist the water logged car, or whatever it was, out of the canal. One sheriff's deputy had already left on another call, so it was just Hal, the frustrated towing guy, and a rookie deputy on the scene.

Once the second truck arrived, the drivers conferred

briefly, selected a plan of attack, and like a pair of diesel gulping synchronized swimmers, they hoisted and dragged the vehicle out of the algae coated water and onto the shoulder.

Weeds, mud, spider web-like green goop, and snails covered the vehicle. But the gold and black U.S. Fish and Wildlife Service seal was plainly visible on the driver's side door. The vehicle belonged to Dean Applegate, who's limp, putrefying body could be seen hanging upside down in the driver's seat.

"Jesus Christ," the rookie cop said with a gasp. "There's a *guy* in there!"

"Usually is," one of the tow truck drivers said nonchalantly as he walked over to the Explorer and readjusted the hooks so the vehicle could be tipped over onto its wheels. "Sometimes a wife and kids too. Even had one with a dog and a cat."

Hal barely heard the insensitive comments of the hardened tow truck operator since he was so focused on Applegate. *They'd finally found him. But here in a canal? A few miles from home? It just seemed strange. And the guy was even wearing his seat belt!*

The rookie deputy made some notes and called for backup. Then he and Hal made a cursory search of the vehicle, trying to leave everything in place. The deputy had a camera and took a few pictures before opening the doors and windows of the malodorous vehicle.

Suicide crossed Hal's mind immediately. But would someone committing suicide wear a seat belt? An inspection of the body showed no evidence of a bullet wound or other trauma. His right arm was at a funny angle— broken, maybe—but that was the only thing that appeared grossly abnormal. They'd have to wait for the autopsy to be

---

sure. Even the tow truck men said this looked like a guy who had drowned.

Then Hal noticed something stuck to the ceiling of the Explorer. It was a piece of colorful paper. Bright yellow. With columns of words and numbers in black type. Hal recognized it as a stock list. An animal dealer's inventory. And the words **"Dade Reptiles and Exotics"** were centered boldly at the top of the page.

Chuck Wickler knew he had to release Baker soon. All they had on him was piloting a boat without a life preserver and registration card—hardly felonious acts. In fact, he would be free to go the next morning unless they had some hard evidence implicating him in the disappearance of Mantis, and it was already almost five o'clock in the afternoon. Baker hadn't asked for a court appointed attorney yet. But if he ever did get one, and the lawyer found out that Wickler had held Baker over two days without just cause, any case against the big quiet fellow could be substantially weakened.

Wickler had Baker taken from his cell to the questioning room. "Now listen, Bobby. I'm gonna have to let you go tomorrow. But that won't bother me much. 'Cause if we turn up some solid evidence linking you with the disappearance of Hunter Ivan, then things are gonna be real bad for you—much worse than if you tell us what you know right now. Heck, admitting to something might take ten, twenty years off any time you would do for a murder wrap. But it's all up to you. I'm giving you a chance. And it's your last one."

Baker was silent, but he no longer just focused on the pale wall behind Wickler. He actually glanced about the room as Wickler spoke. And the *No body, no murder* mantra was barely audible in his mind. As Wickler ranted on like a father scolding a deaf child, Baker stuffed his right hand into his front pants pocket and stroked the folded magazine article he had torn from a recent issue of the *Florida Naturalist*. The magazine had been placed in his cell with several other periodicals. The feel of the crinkled glossy paper put him at ease, and he just hoped Wickler would go away so he could pull the comforting words and pictures from the security of his pocket, and reread the story that had captured his soul in the jail cell.

"You've got the whole night to think it over, Baker," Wickler said as he stood up and started a slow walk around the small room. "Soon as I leave here I'm headin' straight back to my office. Gonna check on my sources and see what new leads have turned up. Who knows, we may *already* have the goods on you. Cooperating with us now will make things so much easier. Trust me."

With no response from the suspect, Wickler signaled for the deputy to take Baker back to his cell.

Once the deputy had locked the iron door to the cell and walked away down the hall, Baker pulled the wad of paper from his pocket. The six page article, as if alive, happily unfolded without the pressure of Baker's pocket lining. The rounded block letters at the top of the first page were colored light green and spelled out the title: **SEA TURTLES, A Cornucopia of Issues** by Dr. Peter C. H. Pritchard. There were beautiful pictures of leatherbacks, ridleys, and greens in the wild as well as photos of harvested eggs and stuffed hawksbill curios. It was these photographs that first grabbed Baker's attention as he flipped through the magazine.

The story reviewed the natural history of those sea turtle species found in Florida and Caribbean waters, and highlighted the numerous threats to sea turtle populations, most of which were directly attributable to man. Scientists and volunteers working to save sea turtles were also featured. It took Baker over an hour to get through the text the first time. Now he could do it in about thirty minutes. Each time through he became more interested—more fascinated—more mesmerized. And more guilty. Guilty about the robbed nests. Guilty about the dead hatchlings. Guilty about Hunter Ivan. And guilty for not making more of his life.

Baker knew that Applegate had planned to sell the baby turtles to an animal dealer in Miami, and according to Hess, that's exactly what he did before splitting with the money. It was certainly possible that at least *some* of the baby turtles were still in Miami. A mere seventy miles away and the only place in the world where Baker knew his way around.

TWENTY-THREE

THE TWENTY-SOMETHING GRADUATE STUDENT WHO AN-
swered the phone rolled her eyes in a slow arc as she
pressed the receiver firmly against her abdomen. The
steady clinking in Hal's ear was caused by the student's
belly button ring which, like a child playing hopscotch,
gently skipped among the small holes in the mouthpiece
each time she breathed. "Oh Dr. Phiiii—lllon. Officer
Noble's on the phone."

Lydia hit the save button on her computer key pad
and hurried over to the amused Gen-Xer, eager to retrieve
the phone.

"Hal! How's it going?" Lydia said as she twirled away
from the eavesdropping student, clutching the long
twisted cord in her free hand.

"Listen, Lydia. How soon can you get to Miami?"
There was an urgency to Hal's voice that she hadn't heard
before.

"Well. I could probably get things wrapped up here
and—"

Hal cut her off, "It's real important. Might involve the

Pavilion Key ridleys. I'll call you on your mobile in fifteen minutes and explain everything."

"Uh. All right, I guess," Lydia was surprised but processed Hal's words quickly. "I'm on my way."

Hal didn't want to lose another precious minute. They were probably already too late—at least if his hunch about Applegate was correct.

Dade Reptiles and Exotics was a place with a bad history. The current owner, Winslow Greene, had chalked up over fifty thousand dollars in fines over the past five years for illegally selling protected and endangered species— primarily birds and reptiles. His one-time partner, Eddie De Werld, was doing a two-year stint at a medium security joint in Tallahassee for selling Galapagos tortoises and marine iguanas to a collector in Europe. A blatant violation of the Convention on International Trade in Endangered Species (CITES), and the Lacey Act, a federal statute that allows U.S. law enforcement agencies to prosecute violators of international wildlife laws. The animals had been taken from Isabela Island in a bold raid staged by Ecuadoran Nationals. The South Americans were eventually caught, sung like tree frogs, and fingered Dade Reptiles as the buyer. The U.S. Fish and Wildlife folks got to Greene first, who turned state's evidence in the case, tossing his buddy to the feds like a rat to a hungry snake. For his contribution, Greene was allowed to stay in business, but was warned that spot inspections of his facility, invoices, and airplane manifests would become more frequent.

The exploding captive reptile hobby made risk taking worth while. Greene could cover a year's worth of Fish and Wildlife fines with a single shipment. And his accountant had even figured out a way to deduct the fines from the company's annual income tax forms. They were merely a cost of doing business.

If Applegate *were* mixed up with Greene, it might explain the fate of the ridley eggs, Hal reasoned. On the other hand, the stock list might have simply been in Applegate's vehicle because he was purchasing herps from Greene for his private collection. Either way, a visit to Greene's facility would probably help with the case.

Hal didn't notify the U.S. Fish and Wildlife people of his plans to inspect Dade Reptiles and Exotics. Partly because of the potential conflict of interest involving the Applegate case. And partly because there was no guarantee that if Applegate was somehow involved with Greene, he was acting alone. The National Marine Fisheries Service was out too. They only had jurisdiction over protected marine species in the ocean or along the intertidal zone— not in a home, garage, or warehouse.

Hal made two calls as he sped towards Miami along the Trail. One was to the Ranger station, telling them he was headed to Miami, the other was to Lydia. He brought her up to speed, and informed her that she might be helpful in hatchling or egg identification—if that became necessary.

After making the calls, Hal had about ten minutes to think quietly when the cell phone in the Blazer chirped to life. It was Jasper.

"Know that guy you picked up the other day drivin' around in the Zodiac with no clue? Well—he's in one of them pictures posted down at the sheriff's substation."

"Yes, Jasper. I heard that yesterday," Hal sighed. "Is that why you're calling me on the car phone?"

"Partly. And the other partly to tell ya that in the picture, the guy's diggin' a hole on Pavilion Key."

Hal was silent for a second. "Pavilion Key! You *sure* it's Pavilion?"

"Hal—"

"Okay. Okay. You're sure. Listen. I need to go check something out in Miami. Should be back in a few hours. Where's the guy now?"

"Far as I know, still in jail."

"Good. When I get back, you and I are heading over to the substation. You can tell what you know about the picture, and the deputies and I'll have a talk with Zodiac-man."

"Roger that. You know where I'll be," Jasper said eagerly.

This new bit of information made Hal less suspicious of Greene, but the slimy animal broker was still worth checking out. After all, Zodiac-man would be back at the substation, safely in a cell, with the rent fully paid.

Unfortunately, Jasper wasn't privy to the fact that Baker's lease had run out early that morning. It was one of the few times he had provided Hal with misinformation.

Hal met Lydia at the predetermined spot, a Dunkin Donuts located on the Tamiami Trail in West Miami, four miles from the large free-standing sheet metal building that was Dade Reptiles and Exotics. The discolored building with its mashed gutters and flaky paint was just a toad's hop from Miami International Airport.

Hal's plan was simple and straightforward. Lydia would remain in the Blazer. If Hal found anything suspicious, or if Greene was uncooperative, Hal would summon the Miami Police for a full search of the place. If an on-the-spot identification was needed, Lydia, an expert and authority on sea turtles, would be right there for the job.

The image of the Wildlife officer and his female companion parked in front of the warehouse was drinking-water clear on the television monitor. The high resolution video camera and its asphalt-entombed vehicle-sensitive pressure plate were paying for themselves again. Greene didn't waste any time trying to read the unwelcome visitor's lips as they sat and chatted, belted to their seats. Like a wild carnivore hunting prey, he slipped from a side door and into the waning Miami sun, which cast an orange glow about his corpulent, sweaty form. Then he inched along the metallic wall of his building, reading the rivets and raised aluminum seams with his large rounded back like a fat blind hand passing over braille. In a moment he could see the wildlife officer opening the outer door to the front of the warehouse. The woman was still sitting quietly in the Blazer.

Greene had tried to keep up with the Applegate vanishing episode—but the Miami papers only ran the story for a couple of days—and his poaching contacts in the field had no information about the missing U.S. Fish and Wildlife agent. If he never heard from Applegate again, it certainly wouldn't hurt his feelings.

The first Pavilion ridleys had hatched a week ago. The eggs from the second nest produced thirty-five hatchlings two days later. Young turtles were pulling themselves from the sand in the third bucket even now. A few of the hatchlings were deformed with abnormally short flippers—one even had two heads. The majority looked pretty good despite having some trouble treading the thin fresh water Greene had provided them with. The entire group of new ridleys were crammed into a fifty-five gallon aquarium with a single, primitive box filter that had long since given up the battle with the copious amount of nitrogenous waste the hatchlings produced.

Seven of the turtles had already been shipped to a black market dealer in Kyoto, Japan—stuffed into newspaper that lined the styrofoam boxes of a green iguana shipment.

Fines and wrist-slaps didn't phase Winslow Greene, but dealing endangered sea turtles, with his record, guaranteed some jail time. And that he couldn't afford.

Lydia had no time to react . . . save for the widening of her eyelids as Greene grabbed her by the neck through the open window. With the fingers of his right hand clutching her throat like fire ant pincers on soft toe skin, Greene used his free hand to open the door of the Blazer. "Any sound at all, 'cept breathing, and I tear out your windpipe. Clear?"

Lydia nodded slowly.

Greene maintained his grip on the young professor and pulled her from the seat. "Good. Now get your ass outta this car and walk as fast as you can in front of me."

Lydia shuffled away from the Blazer with Greene leading from behind as if they were engaged in a bizarre kind of forced dance. His large calloused hand remained locked to her neck, and in less than fifteen seconds, he was pushing her through the side door of the warehouse. Once in the building, they made two quick turns, passed through an open but darkened doorway, and stopped short before a steel door covered with cold gray paint.

"You don't look like no wildlife officer," Greene said as he groped at a wooden shelf with his left hand and secured a thick role of duct tape. "What's your story?"

Greene didn't look like a guy to lie to, so Lydia told

him that she taught biology and did research on sea turtles at FAU.

"Kinda thought that's why you two showed up." Using his teeth and powerful fingers, Greene liberated a twelve inch piece of tape that he flattened over Lydia's mouth and ears. Now with both hands free, he ripped off an even longer piece, which he doubled over the first swatch and continued applying to her head until her lips were flat against her teeth. Then he forced her hands behind her back at the waist and spun the entire roll of duct tape around her wrists five times before tearing the roll free with a quick, downward jerk.

Lydia thought about kicking her assailant in the crotch, but before she could get her feet set, the gray door flung open and Greene's powerful hand ramrodded her into a dimly lit room. There was a large water-filled aquarium perched atop a rusty metal stand in one corner and a few cardboard and styrofoam boxes scattered about the rest of the peeling linoleum floor. The muffled buzz of an air pump filled the stale air.

With Lydia lying on her belly, Greene mummified her feet and ankles with the rest of the duct tape. Then he said in a low whisper, "I'll be right back. There's a game warden loose in my place and I'm gonna catch him." Lydia remained helpless on the floor as the door closed quietly shut and Greene's footsteps faded away down the hall.

Hal had knocked on the screen door which separated the main part of the warehouse from the small anteroom where he stood, and hearing no response, he cautiously opened the flimsy, unlocked door and entered the warehouse.

"Anybody here?" he said in a loud voice which was a few decibels short of a yell. "Anyone around?" Hal continued to walk slowly through the warehouse where cages and crates crammed with iguanas, snakes, and tortoises seemed to be everywhere. Haphazardly sandwiched between the reptiles were filthy, feces-encrusted aquariums crawling with huge black scorpions, tarantulas, hissing cockroaches, and half-dead crickets.

The thirty-three ounce aluminum baseball bat which struck Hal in the back of the head punched his brain from one side of his skull to the other. Only a few millimeters in each direction, but the trauma and subsequent swelling were enough to put his central nervous system into a temporary coma. Winslow Greene stood over Hal, who was unconscious and heaped in a leg and arm pile on the floor. Blood trickled from Hal's right ear and his breathing was slow and deliberate. Several drops of sweat succumbed to the pull of gravity and dropped from Greene's downturned nose onto the shirt of the injured wildlife officer. Greene's eyes were on fire and a thin smile began to part the unkempt hair of his mustache and beard. "That outta hold the bastard."

Greene walked over to a packing table where styrofoam boxes, plastic bags, rubber bands, and zip-ties were kept. He grabbed several of the zip-ties and knelt down on the rough cement floor where Hal lay. Then, using his bulky fingers to apply excessive force, he quickly secured Hal's ankles and wrists with the irreversible nylon restraints.

Within minutes he had dragged Hal face down like a sack of rock salt to the locked gray door which imprisoned Lydia. Greene opened the door, checked to be sure Lydia was still bound on her belly, and dragged Hal the final few feet into the room. Then he let Hal's legs drop to the floor with a blunt crack.

Greene knew Lydia was still conscious and felt he needed to give her an explanation before he killed the pair. "If you're any kinda religious—start prayin'. I ain't never killed before. No person anyway. But this is too big. You got hooked up with the wrong feller, lady. This Noble jerk's been hasslin' folks tryin' to make a livin' off a critters for years. I ain't sorry killin' him. You. Well. It won't be as easy. But I'm a survivor." Then he left the room, closing the door behind him.

Lydia was crying with fear. A fear she had never known. "Hal! Hal! Hal, can you hear me? Hal. Please. Hal. Wake up!" But the duct tape filtered her desperate words into an incoherent mumble.

Lydia then began to shimmy, on her abdomen a centimeter at a time, toward Hal who was lying face down about ten feet away. Between each painful gyration of her body, she called Hal's name with a guttural moan, and each time there was no answer.

Greene checked the video monitor, and seeing no vehicles or pedestrian activity, he went outside and climbed into Hal's patrol vehicle. Using the keys he had liberated from the unconscious Game and Fish officer, he started the Blazer and drove to the back of the warehouse where the ground-level loading dock was located. He stopped the Blazer, got out, and quickly flipped through a three digit combination, unlocking a stocky padlock which secured the corrugated steel garage door. After opening the door, he drove the Blazer inside and closed the door behind him. He made his way through the dimly lit warehouse to the front door, he locked it, and took a seat by the video monitor. A quick glance at his watch showed five fifteen P.M.

An hour passed. The parking lot in front of the warehouse remained quiet. And a soft bumping noise in the middle of Greene's surveillance appeared to be nothing more than a male redfoot tortoise falling off of its unwilling mate.

The time had come to kill the intruders. Greene pulled a nine millimeter Baretta semiautomatic pistol from a filing cabinet in his office, chambered a round, and walked down the hallway which lead to the gray door. Unlocking and opening the door, Greene noted that the woman was now lying adjacent to Noble, who still appeared to be unconscious. Lydia looked up, and upon seeing Greene with the Baretta in hand, screamed Hal's name again. Still no response.

"He ain't never wakin' up little lady. And it's just as well—'cause he won't have to see you get shot." Then Greene pulled a switch blade from his pocket, sliced through the sticky gray gag around Lydia's face, and ripped a flap of tape free, exposing her lips.

"Please don't kill us," Lydia pleaded. "It's not worth it. Please, please think about what you're doing."

"Oh. I've thought about it. And I don't have no choice," Greene said. "These baby turtles brought you here—and they're gonna take me away. 'Course if I get caught, they take me to the wrong place. But when I finish sellin' 'em, it's life at the beach for this old redneck. So you understand why I gotta do this. I promise it'll be quick." Greene then pulled an old cloth snake bag from his pocket and wrapped it around Lydia's head, covering her eyes.

Greene raised the pistol and took aim at Lydia's head, which was turned sideways, pressed close to Hal's waist. She continued to plead with Greene for mercy and tears began to soak through the makeshift blindfold.

Just as he pulled the trigger, Lydia turned her head quickly towards the floor and the bullet hit her in the left

194

cheek bone, scattering flesh, blood, and bone fragments onto Hal's back, which continued to heave slow and regular, like a patient on a mechanical respirator.

Greene surveyed his failed execution. "Now why'd ya have to make it hard on yourself? I didn't mean for you to feel no pain. Let's try it again." This time Greene placed the barrel of the hand gun no more than twelve inches from Lydia's head.

At the moment he began to squeeze the trigger, the cool, smooth aluminum of a golf club-like snake hook sliced through Greene's carotid artery and drilled a ragged hole in his trachea. The Baretta dipped, his grip on the weapon weakened, and he turned just in time to catch the full force of Bobby Baker's dirt-caked boot in his mouth.

Greene fell to the ground, blood spurting from his neck in regular, rhythmic bursts. His torn trachea made it difficult to breathe, and his open-mouthed gasps only succeeded in sucking several dislodged teeth into the main bronchi of his lungs.

In a matter of seconds, Greene went into cardiovascular shock and passed out. He was dead in five minutes—nearly a gallon of his clotting blood covered the dull, plastic floor.

While Greene hemorrhaged, Baker used a pocket knife to slash through the duct tape binding Lydia's ankles. Then he stood her up, pressed a napkin he had pulled from his pocket against the wound on her face, and walked her to the corner by the turtle-filled aquarium.

Hal was next. Baker dragged his limp body away from the growing pool of blood and propped him up next to Lydia. He left Hal's shackles in place.

"I'll go get some water," Baker said to the still blindfolded Lydia. "Be right back."

Baker returned in a minute with a large feeding bowl full of water. He used some to clean the wound on Lydia's face and left the bowl on the floor next to Hal. "You can use this to wake him up."

Convinced that Hal and Lydia were safe, Baker walked over to the aquarium, and stared at the struggling creatures within. He seemed entranced by the small prisoners. His eyes followed one turtle for a moment. Then another. And then another. But he remained stationery. A single index finger gently touched the glass separating him from the tiny reptiles. After a minute he returned to Lydia, cut the duct tape binding her wrists, and marched quickly across the room, disappearing behind the gray door.

Lydia snatched the folded snake bag from her head and splashed the animal bowl water on Hal's face. The drenching started Hal's motor and he moaned softly.

"Oh Hal. My God. Are you all right?" Lydia said, holding Hal's face in her hands.

"Well. I guess so. What the heck's going on?"

Lydia pointed to the mound of bleeding fat on the floor. "That guy tried to kill us. Shoot us. I was sure we were dead. Then some other man. Who left I think. He saved us. Saved our lives."

The haze began to lift from Hal's brain and he realized that Greene was dead—killed by an anonymous savior.

It was time to find a phone.

TWENTY-FOUR

"HOW'S THAT BEAUTIFUL FACE OF YOURS?" HAL SAID AS he walked into the hospital room carrying a modest bouquet of flowers and a few trendy get well balloons.

"You tell me," Lydia replied. "I hope it looks better than it feels."

Lydia required reconstructive surgery to repair the damage caused by Greene's bullet. The permanent scarring would be minimal.

"Well. We located the Kyoto ridleys," Hal said, hoping the good news would lift Lydia's spirits. "Japanese agents had to go door to door to get a few of them, but they're all accounted for and on their way back to Miami."

"That's a relief. How 'bout the ones from the warehouse?"

"All fine. They're keeping them at the Miami Seaquarium until we can bring 'em back to Pavilion Key.

"How many total?"

"Eighty-nine. Including the seven from Japan," Hal said. "I'm taking them back to the beach this weekend. Was hoping you could make it. Figured you might want to take some pictures for that publication."

Lydia smiled and tears washed her eyes. "I'll be there."

Lydia Phillon did publish on the Pavilion Key ridleys, and even made Jasper and Hal coauthors on the paper. The National Marine Fisheries Service, U.S. Fish and Wildlife Service, and the National Parks Service all cooperated in granting Pavilion Key special protection as the only permanent nesting site for the Kemp's ridley sea turtle in the United States.

Bobby Baker's decision to stake out Winslow Greene's place over several other area exotic animal importers was pure luck. In fact, after observing the Dade Reptiles and Exotics warehouse for several hours from behind a large bush, Baker was ready to knock on the front door and ask for a tour when Hal and Lydia pulled up. Sneaking into the warehouse was easy once Greene drove Hal's Blazer around back. But staying hidden and quiet was a bit of a challenge for the lumbering ex-con.

The Miami police were unable to solve Winslow Greene's murder, and six months after the investigation started, the file was placed at the bottom of a very large stack of similar cases. The Greene killing wasn't exactly a top priority for an understaffed and overworked south Florida homicide unit.

Dean Applegate's death was ultimately ruled an accident, and after some political squabbling among several U.S. Fish and Wildlife Service or USF&WS administrators and accountants, Susan Applegate was awarded a modest pension despite the discovery of Applegate's various illegal activities. While not enough to comfortably support a family of three, Susan was able to keep clothes on the kids and a car on the road, with free housing as a resident condominium supervisor—on Marco Island.

TWENTY-FIVE

AUGUST, A YEAR LATER:

The ten-foot swells tossed happy surfers and ocean foam about the dynamic shallows which waxed and waned over the Topsail Island sand. A hundred miles to the southeast, Hurricane Bonnie, a big fat category three storm, was stuffing water and wind toward the vulnerable North Carolina barrier island.

Nearly eight hundred miles to the south, Detective Chuck Wickler was flipping lazily through the Hunter Ivan file, which at a year old and void of fresh leads, was ready for the stale-case filing cabinet.

The catfish ring had been sent to Ivan's family months ago. Baker had vanished like a startled bonefish. And no other sign of Mantis had ever been found. In fact, the last bits of his bone and gristle had been consumed by ravenous crustaceans just weeks before, and a few resourceful marine worms had used his teeth and hair to help contruct their protective tubes.

Mantis was now a small but dynamic piece of the Everglades ecosystem he so admired and cherished.

Wickler fumbled among the papers and photographs until he found the picture of Mantis in Flamingo. The care-free optimism and inner peace were still splashed across the loner's face. "Poor bastard," he muttered at the flat image. "Probably just part of the food chain by now."

"Another clutch moved to safety," Karen Banza, the thirty-year-old director of the Topsail Sea Turtle Program said proudly. Banza supervised over a hundred mostly re-tired volunteers who patrolled the beaches protecting and identifying sea turtle nests during the summer and early fall. Recently, she was able to raise enough money through donations to hire a full-time staff person. She and her dedi-cated assistant were moving the last loggerhead nests to high ground before the pending mandatory evacuation. "No storm surge will wash these eggs away. Ready for the next one?"

"Ready. Just show me where to dig," Billy Becker re-plied, a big grin spreading spots of sand and seawater across his beaming face. "Nothin' feels better than helpin' these critters get into the world."